Rufus
A Haircut

David Selby

Illustrations by Katie Colquitt

Typesetting by Socciones Editoria Digitale
www.socciones.co.uk

Contents

INTRODUCTION

'Rufus Needs A Haircut' was born many years ago. The tales herein are all reworkings of shaggy dog stories I've been fortunate enough to have heard, in some guise or other, and reworked at loose moments, usually quite long moments if truth be known, in many classrooms to many unfortunate students over many years. Much to their chagrin. Rufus, himself, features and as his coat is somewhat shaggy, he became the eponymous hero of the title.

I had considered writing the tales a few years ago, but it was only during the 'lockdown' that I actually sat myself down to put pen to paper. There was something about a dormant time, not quite knowing (and still far from certain) as to how it might end that seemed to correlate with a shaggy dog story. I also wanted to try to give something back to some of the very many people who had done so much more than their duty to help our society. Rufus' own tale reveals my thoughts on 'celebrity'. The people who really deserve our time, admiration and gratitude are, as in times when there is no pandemic, those who look after others, putting them before themselves. I earnestly hope that over time our deep appreciation of such people remains. We champion our NHS, rather than decry it. We look after our elderly, rather than overlook them. And we value and reward those who look after others in whatever capacity.

In recognition of their extraordinary work, I am donating £1.50 from the sale of each book to the NHS Charities Together. I don't like stating something in such a way as it sounds rather pious and presumptuous. However, if that fact encourages anyone to purchase 'Rufus' then it will have been worth the stating.

The importance of our mental health and wellbeing has been something raised far more in our society over recent years. The enforced lockdown, resulting in isolation and separation for many who could ill afford it and also many who may have been far less aware that it would affect them adversely, has highlighted the importance of good mental health and support for that goal.

A shaggy dog story does test patience and, if successful, manages at best, a rather painful wince from the poor recipient. There is an inherent, irreverent and totally self-deprecating avenue to be followed when considering the well-being of anyone who has had the misfortune of listening to one. That, in no way whatsoever, belittles the importance of the cause.

Some of these tales name or allude to real people in the public eye. Without them, the stories don't work! I would like to state, I have the utmost respect for all of those familiar names, their work and their art. I sincerely hope they take their inclusion here with the humour and generosity of spirit that I intended when writing these tales.

Words are words. As a continuation in the right order, they tell these tales. But they are enlivened and brightened by the wizardry of the artist, Katie, who is a friend of my daughter, Thalia. Once her artistic talents came to light, Katie was far too polite to decline when asked about the possibility of creating some artwork to support the ramblings. Of course, it meant she had to read them, too. And she **still** did it! I couldn't have hoped for anything like what she has produced.

Finally, I would like to thank my wife, Katherine, for her tireless support and patience typing up my manuscript, editing and proof reading these stories.

I hope you enjoy ruffling the shaggy coat of Rufus and these far-fetched stories.

PROLOGUE

Before you take a tentative step into the stories, may I make some suggestions?

These tales are composed with a view to being read aloud; performed, if you like.

In some there are obvious sound effects. Should you ever decide to read aloud to some willing (or unwilling) listener, I would advise that you attempt the sound effects. Don't be shy – they bring the stories to life! For example, 'The Bloody Red Knight on the Bloody Red Horse' does rap upon the gatehouse door and the door of the monarch on quite a few occasions. On each, the set of responses are very similar. Achieving those sound effects and the tone in the questions and responses is all part of the tale.

Finally, the majority of these stories end with a denouement which might be perceived as, how shall I put it... a touch painful. As you progress towards the (anti)climax, it may be prudent to put some distance between yourself and whomsoever has had the pleasure of you as raconteur. Or, at the very least, make sure there's a quick exit at hand.

Without further ado, I welcome you to the wonderful world of our shaggy dog Rufus and his fictitious friends...

THE LONG LOST BACON TREE
–
SIR WALTER RALEIGH VENTURES OUT

Sir Walter Raleigh has, I believe, lost some of his once iconic lustre over recent generations. Even as a schoolboy, I don't recall receiving much by way of reverential accolades from doting history teachers. Now, of course, the health and fitness concerns of our nation may, in no small part, go some way to explaining our hero's fall from grace (and let me add, right here right now, that this fall will be seen as foolishness and short-sightedness upon our part once his tale has been told here). So eminent should Sir Walter be in our proud nation's annals that he deigns to make a reappearance in this book…

Back to the health and fitness of our nation. A mere 40 years ago, the potato and tobacco were staples of our adult diet… and, from what I remember of my school days, not just the diet of an adult. But the potato has long since been surpassed, first by pasta and then brown rice, quinoa and cous cous (so good, they named… well you get the point).

And tobacco? Long gone are the little vending machines outside the newsagents from which 10 Woodbine or Players No X could be extracted for the price of few old pennies, pre the decimalisation which was the forerunner to our happy and prosperous union with all things European. Tobacco is now hidden away under dark clothing, like some defendant we see on the television being hustled in to stand trial for the heinous crime of mass murder whilst, clearly, already having been convicted in all of our minds. By comparison, our friendly 'spud' has received merely a suspended sentence and can still be seen touting its wares in ever-more flamboyant disguises (Hasselback?!) on the increasing number of reality TV cookery shows that crowd our viewing schedules.

So, Sir Walter. Not that surprising that your legacy, seemingly so certain and steadfast only 50 years ago, has been indelibly tarnished. How fair can it be that the daring adventurer can topple from his pedestal at the vagaries of fashion fads and, admittedly more importantly, progress in medical and health awareness?

But all is not lost! How so? I hear you cry. Well, for the simple reason that our hero was famed for more adventures and quests than simply bringing back the potato and tobacco to our civilised isle. Let me take you back to the Court of Queen Elizabeth I and, to be more precise, one day before her 42nd birthday.

'Bring me Sir Walter,' announced our monarch, in somewhat of a displeased tone.

Sir Walter duly appeared in the quickest of flashes. Word has it that, post his potato and tobacco glory days, he had settled into the pampered life of a courtier and was always very quick to ingratiate himself with the Queen, believing he inhabited a privileged position with her favours. He was about to be shaken out of such reveries.

"Walt," uttered Elizabeth. For it was true that she did incline towards him and such a term of endearment was the manner in which she usually chose to address him.

"Walt, I've been thinking. You don't seem to have done too much over the past few years. For a dashing adventurer you have merely dashed from one liaison to another and have discovered nothing other than a variety of avenues in which to satisfy your rather licentious appetite."

"But Ma'am… I mean Your Majesty…" stammered a clearly shaken Sir Walter. However, he was unable to add to this less-than-convincing opening for his defence, in large part due to the well-held opinion that he was, indeed, somewhat of a ladies' man. He hadn't actually left the court for over three years and his many

4

'discoveries' during this time, whilst undeniably pleasurable, had only resulted in a rather itchy and flaky skin condition on two separate occasions of which he was not inclined to boast. He did try the medicinal qualities of the potato and tobacco but, alas, neither seemed to have the desired effect.

"Put bluntly, Walt, you've been resting on your laurels. It can go on no longer; I need our nation's hero to go off and be, well, heroic," continued the Monarch, who was now finding her rhetoric beginning to flow. "And so, I have decided to send you on a quest. A very personal mission, Walt."

"Ah. Indeed, Ma'am," replied the previously crestfallen Sir Walter, who was now mixing a tone of resignation, concern and (feigned) jubilation on his response… and that cocktail was quite an achievement.

Queen Elizabeth bent down from the throne upon which she was sitting and retrieved a rolled-up parchment. To Sir Walter's eyes it looked old and delicate and when the Queen began to unfurl the parchment, his initial belief was not diminished in any way.

"I have here a hand-drawn image of a plant – a tree, as a matter of fact – which has been stored in the vaults at our Royal Gardens at Kew." At this point in the proceedings she turned her gaze upon Sir Walter whilst still displaying the somewhat spidery image. "Walt, this is the 'Long Lost Bacon Tree'. I want it not to be lost but to be found. And you are just the man to exact this feat."

Sir Walter's initial concern was about to grow into something distinctly more palpable… Worry? No. Fear.

"Walt, as you know, tomorrow is my birthday," Queen Elizabeth, pronounced.

"And may I be the first to offer my hearty congratulations and felicitations," interjected Sir Walter, whilst determining that a bag of his new 'ready salted potato snacks' and a 'pinch of ready rubbed' might not, quite, be a good enough offering for the mean-mooded monarch.

"Thank you... but I'd much rather be greeted with specimens of this strange tree than empty words, Walt." She was clearly in no mood to be budged. "You have one year and one day to complete the quest, returning here on my following birthday with your hard-earned gift. You may take 'The Intrepid' flagship of our navy, and 250 of our best sailors. Should you fail in this quest, Walt, it pains me to say that your head will part company from your shoulders!"

Sir Walter desperately sought for more by way of time, provision and tactics, but his mind, so accustomed to recent leisurely and languid life, could only reply, "Of course, my Queen. What you command shall, as always, be enacted."

Not quite the words he had hoped would come out of his mouth; indeed, he felt it rather surreal, as if someone else had made that proclamation. Some blathering idiot... until, of course he realised that it was he, without a shadow of a doubt, who was the aforementioned blathering idiot.

Hiding his sense of foreboding, Sir Walter took his leave of Queen Elizabeth holding, very carefully, the document which detailed the fabled 'Long Lost Bacon Tree'. He cut a forlorn figure as he took the well-trodden path, down the Palace's corridors to his suite of rooms. The larger-than-life gigolo had been, in almost an instant, replaced by a frightened and fatigued figure.

"What am I to do?" Sir Walter's rhetorical question fell upon deaf ears... as it would. But in the same breath that he had announced his seemingly defeatist attitude, he sprang up and became defiant, 'danger knows full well that Sir Walter is more dangerous than he!" Clearly the recent production of Julius Caesar at court had left its mark on Sir Walter. Of course, the irony that he was (mis)quoting the ill-fated eponymous figure seemed to be lost upon him.

"When the chips are down..." he continued, before becoming lost in glorious imaginings. Almost instantly, he was not thinking of 'chips' in the potato sense – as they were still centuries in the waiting - but unconsciously he had offered us, the reader and listener, a wonderful example of irony.

Within the space of one day, Sir Walter had enlisted and assembled his crew. The Intrepid was piled high with provisions, for this was likely to be a long journey. Sir Walter determined that he would not give details of the quest to his men until they had set sail. He pondered on what words he would employ when galvanising and inspiring those brave sailors.

In truth, he was still deliberating when, one evening two hours out of the port of Folkestone, he faced his crew.

"Men," he began, feeling himself to be fairly safe with such an opening. "Men, we are gathered together, the favoured ones, chosen to secure a goal set by our beloved leader, Queen Elizabeth I. We are to search the known and, if it comes to it, unknown world for evidence of..." Never one to miss an opportunity for dramatic effect, Sir Walter unfurled the document he had been cradling in his arms... "the Long Lost Bacon Tree." To Sir Walter the now-familiar image seemed to have an hypnotic effect upon his charges... when looking back on this moment he chose to recall an audible intake of breath and, remembering when he had first seen the image, he could only concur that the men were of the same mind as he had been…

"Whilst a very strange-looking tree," he resumed, "we will not rest until we have the Long Lost Bacon Tree aboard The Intrepid and then we shall go back to Blighty to be met as heroes. It will be a birthday our Majestic Queen will never forget."

His concluding words were drowned in a sea of cheers from the ecstatic and, in truth, overly optimistic crew.

Time doesn't tell of the very many lands The Intrepid visited. Nor does it detail what welcomes or hostilities were visited upon the brave Sir Walter and his men. What we do know, however, is that they did not, in all their searching, come across any growth remotely resembling the totally unique description of the 'Long Lost Bacon Tree'.

We resume our tale, as history records, with a most despondent and dejected Sir Walter. Doomed to be setting sail for England's shores and a reception so out of character with anything he had previously experienced. And so, it was that at early evening he ordered the anchor to be dropped a mere 200 yards from the shore of the uncharted island. The sun dropped nearly on the horizon casting the whole land mass into what appeared to be a large silhouette. In truth, the island couldn't have mustered more than a mile in width. How deep was it? No-one knew; indeed no-one knows to this day. But, shame on my narrative know-how. I must not reveal any of the ending before we arrive at it as did Sir Walter… Suffice to say, the island was, at once, both beautiful and strangely unsettling.

The gloomy adventurer took up his telescope and scanned the horizon. Such was his pessimism that the island itself was last to be viewed. His rather bored glance was immediately halted; time seemed to slow and even stop as Sir Walter realised what he was looking at. And as it sometimes does, it gradually restarted and began to tick to its normal beat. It was, of course, oblivious to the fact that Sir Walter had frantically dashed to his cabin, retrieved his prized document and returned so as to be able to confirm his belief. Trying to unfurl the document while looking through the telescope was a very difficult task and one which found Sir Walter in a variety of contorted positions….Eventually he gained the ability to look at what was in front of him… the parchment and the reality. The outline was one and the same!

Again he found himself dashing to his cabin to secure the image safely. Then, with a whoop of delight, he raced back to the deck and promptly sounded the ship's bell to call all hands on deck. He was breathless in his excitement, but once the men could understand his message they followed his pointing arm and gazed upon the outline of a tree which seemed to be waving at them, beckoning them to come ashore and secure it as their prize.

The thought of sleep and waiting until morning could not be countenanced. Sir Walter gave order for two of the five sailing boats, which hung to the bowels of The Intrepid, to be lowered and for 50 men in each boat to row to shore.

"Men, be careful. The light will soon be gone and this island is uncharted. Look after each other. Find out if the island can sustain life; is it inhabited and, most important of all, bring back evidence that this wonderful specimen we have all seen is, indeed, the 'Long Lost Bacon Tree'. Sir Walter's voice shook with emotion as he gave word for them to row. "Return by this time tomorrow; we shall sound a musket three times, one half hour before you should be reunited with us. Go. And may God's peace keep you and speed

9

you on your way."

The two boats slowly made their way to the island; the occupants singing and shouting, such was their jubilation. The boats they dragged high upon the shore and with a turn and a wave to all aboard The Intrepid, they separated into groups of their dividing and embarked upon their search.

Night fell and a quietness descended. Sir Walter cut a distracted figure, unable to rest, he paced the deck, excitement and anxiety battling within him. Just before midnight those awake on The Intrepid heard the first sounds. At first, they were low and gave the impression of a creature, or creatures, moaning. This sound was then punctuated by infrequent bursts of a higher-pitched shouting. And now it sounded more like the voices of men, but no-one could be sure it was the call of their comrades. The shouts became more frequent, seemingly by sounding some kind of alarm. But of what were they warning? It was when the first scream was heard that those aboard The Intrepid, all now wide awake, were certain that some terrible fate was befalling those who had set foot upon the island. Screams pierced the night air and sounds so unfamiliar, yet still as terrifying, continued until just before the sun hinted its arrival by way of casting an azure streak on the previously black waters. All fell quiet. Not a sound could be heard. Those aboard The Intrepid looked at each other in alarm, unable to put a voice to their fears, but as the dawn exposed them, their faces told of the horrors they had heard and the terrors they had imagined.

The day passed silently but seemed unbearably long as the appointed time for the reconnoitre approached. The two rowing boats lay on the shore as they had been left. The musket was duly fired, but none aboard The Intrepid expected to be greeted with a response from the island. Not a sight was seen nor a sound heard of the men. The island had claimed them.

Sir Walter gathered his men together. Now was the time to unify them. "Men," he said, on what had become a customary opening to any of his orations. "Men, I fear some terrible fate has befallen our brave comrades. It is our duty to find out what has happened. To see if I am misguided in this belief of tragedy. To find out if any are still alive and need our help. To be wary of any who would do us harm...."

At this point, Sir Walter's voice tailed off as his gaze was met by the lonely silhouette which seemed to pick out The Intrepid as it beckoned its occupants ashore by ruffling its branches in a wave of a welcome. "And we must have evidence of our discovery of the 'Long Lost Bacon Tree'."

His fellow sailors nodded in unison, each equally bewitched by the enticing arms of welcome. When Sir Walter asked for 100 volunteers he had all of those on board, 149 sailors and the ship's boy, step forward to affirm their allegiance to the task. They were not cowed; they were strong and resolute.

One hundred chosen, they descended and, having been given the exact same instructions and guidance as their predecessors, but with an added word of caution, they pushed away from The Intrepid. It took just under 15 minutes for the first boat to make shore, closely followed by its twin. On this occasion, no hearty carousing left their lips, but the sailors merely turned to signal their safe arrival and then departed, more warily, in their pre-determined groups.

As on the night before, all was quiet until just before midnight. Indeed, some believed it to be too quiet. It was providence, not even whispering, but foreshadowing another night of pain, anguish and terror.

Sir Walter had not rested at all and the pain he felt was etched on his face. He was powerless to prevent what was occurring little more than 200 yards from him.

The moans, cries and screams were just as the listeners had heard before.

Knowledge of the previous night did not lessen their scope for horror. Whilst they sounded the same, they still had the capacity to reveal individual suffering. Those aboard The Intrepid were tormented and tortured by the harrowing fate of their fellow seafarers.

Dawn brought no relief; just the agonising wait until the musket was fired. Sir Walter knew, as did his men, this was but a feeble gesture. Hoping against any kind of hope.

Visibly shaken, voice trembling, Sir Walter conceded to the inevitable. They had lost 200 brave fellows. Their own fate was looking increasingly sealed. But Sir Walter would not lie down and die in a manner which gave up the fight.

"My brave, brave men," he began – in a slight departure from the norm, but one which he hoped may signal a change to their fortunes. "It would seem that our fellows have met with a most terrible and unkind fate. We cannot be certain, but I fear that we will not see them again in this world." Sir Walter halted as if he, too, was acknowledging only now the enormity of his words. And, in so doing, he roused himself and, looking each sailor in the eye, he cried. "Men, we owe it to our brave companions to determine what foul deed befell them, if that has been their fate. There may be survivors; we may bring our comrades home. Or we may bury them. Whichever, they need us."

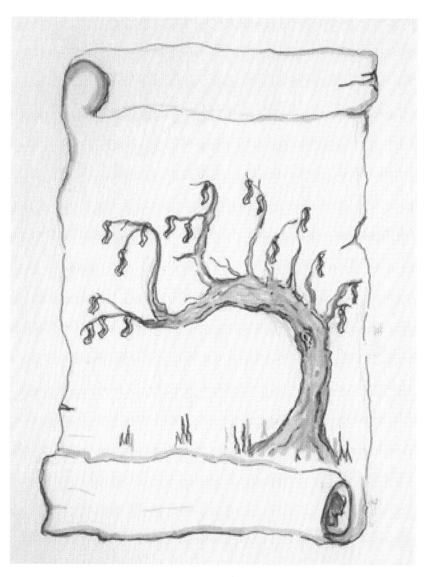

At this point, a cold breeze blew across their faces; all aboard The Intrepid turned from it to see the silhouette of the tree bowing against the direction of the wind. It seemed to be imploring them to come to it, to rescue it, perhaps? That it was communicating to them, no-one had any doubt.

"The remaining 49 of you will board the last, solitary rowing boat and, with great stealth, approach the island. You will seek out the whereabouts and condition of our companions. Discover what has happened on this so treacherous of islands. And, of course, bring news and evidence of our quest... the Long, Lost Bacon Tree. Good luck, men!"

A muted, yet defiant crew boarded the single rowing boat, leaving only Sir Walter and the ship's boy with the unenviable and, quite frankly, impossible task of sailing her home between them. Both figures stood, silent and stock still as they watched 'the 49' disembark upon the shore and disappear into the gathering gloom. And disappear is exactly what they did. They were never to be seen alive again and, perhaps it was their moans, cries and screams that Sir Walter and the Ship's Boy covered their ears in vain attempts to prevent their being heard. Who can say for sure?

The night passed slowly; quietness descended as the previous two nights, shortly before dawn. Once the sun had climbed the first few steps of its oft-repeated journey, Sir Walter could bear it no longer.

"They're dead; massacred; all gone!" he cried, shaking the startled Ship's Boy by the shoulders. "We are broken and defeated." And with those words the tree on the island seemed to nod in agreement, swaying and sashaying to a rhythm of life which no longer was echoed in the pulse of the sailors. Where once it had seemed to implore Sir Walter, it now looked to taunt and ridicule him.

He snapped. This valiant, death-defying adventurer snapped.

"Boy!" he cried, arguably in the same vein as his earlier addresses, but the fact it was in the singular and referred to someone not yet in the flush of his youth served only to add more poignancy to the heart-breaking situation in which the two companions now found themselves. "Boy. You must swim ashore. Alone. Seek out your fellows and bring back word as to what has happened to them. And..." Sir Walter turned puce with indignation and rage as he faced his long-limbed nemesis on the island, waving its branches as if to mock him, "...bring me back that tree. I must have the 'Long Lost Bacon Tree'.

"Go now. Straight away. I shall fire the musket myself in six hours' time to signal your return. Your lone presence may well bring success where the might of many has failed."

With that he hugged the boy, planting a fatherly kiss upon his forehead, before helping him down the rope ladder whose final rung left a matter of inches before the cold of the water below it.

The boy was a strong swimmer and soon made the shore. In a gesture to his master and commander, he turned and saluted before disappearing.

"A brave, brave boy," were the words Sir Walter articulated to the air and he repeated them throughout the next six hours. Not a sight nor sound came from the boy. There were no moans, cries or screams. Just silence.

The musket bellowed into the quiet, but was met by only the faintest of echoes. The final 30 minutes passed so very slowly, painfully slowly. Sir Walter scanned the shoreline for any sign of movement, but it would appear to have been to no avail.

He had given up all hope and had resigned himself to going down with his ship, when he thought he saw... no, surely not.... but, yes, there it was again. A slight splashing in the water not far from the shore.

15

Very slowly, agonisingly slowly, the splashing approached The Intrepid. And as the source of the movement came into view, he realised that it was the Ship's Boy. His swimming stroke was no longer that of the lithe athlete who cut the water so crisply on his outward journey. This was distorted, ungainly and delivered with a maximum of effort. Gradually, inexorably, and painfully slowly, he reached the ladder and Sir Walter could now see the level of his discomfort. His right collar bone protruded through his flesh and two of his ribs sought to keep it company. The boy's left leg had suffered appalling gashes and his kneecap was twisted to what appeared to be an impossible angle. Despite the best effort of the waves, blood smeared his body. His face was a picture of abject misery and suffering, swollen and bruised. He clung to the ladder with his left arm, the only part of his anatomy which seemed to have been spared. His screams of pain rent the air and so appalled Sir Walter, he wept openly.

He brought the boy to him, clasping him close, which served only to increase the young lad's pain, if that were possible.

"Sir, Sir," but he could say no more before losing consciousness.

Sir Walter lay him down gently and from his jacket pocket produced a bottle of rum. Lifting the boy's head he bought the bottle to his lips and ensured he drank. Coughing and retching, the boy was brought back to the horror of his salvation.

"Sir, the pain. The 'orror," before once again, blacking out.

Sir Walter repeated this medicine and the response was immediate and the same. This time the adventurer spoke first.

"My brave, brave boy. You are back and safe with me. Please tell me, where are my men?"

The boy turned his head to Sir Walter which, in itself, was quite a feat as it had been at a most unnatural angle.

"Sir... they're dead. All dead. Slaughtered. It was 'orrible." The tears rolled down his cheeks as his words tumbled out.

"No survivors? Not one?" gaped an incredulous Sir Walter.

"None, Sir." And with that the boy closed his eyes.

Sir Walter, torn between horror, pity and rage, looked up only for his eyes to be met by the tree, still waving at him. Still telling him it was there. Still offering the same promise it made to him when he had first clapped eyes upon it. Biting his tongue, holding back the bile, he whispered to the semi-conscious child who lay in his arms. "Boy. The tree? Is it... is it the 'Long Lost Bacon Tree'?"

The young fellow opened his right eye as far as the swollen lid allowed before replying, in a hushed voice.

"No, Sir. It was an 'ambush."

A YOUNG LIFE CRISIS

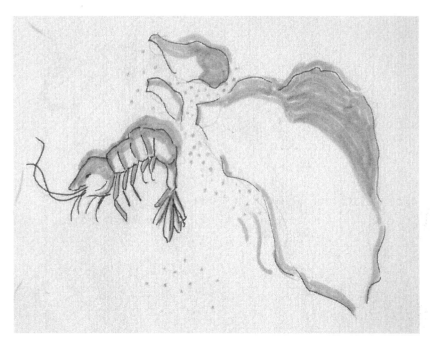

Remember those halcyon days? The never-ending summers of your youth? The sunshine all day, your only care was where and when the next ice cream would appear. A bucket and spade, a bat and ball, and the chance to race into the cool, refreshing water and jump the waves… Well, perhaps a little romanticised as rain like stair rods and a murky sea which would turn you a strange colour and odour, as well as contributing to hypothermia, is not quite the way we tend to look back, is it?

But the rockpools… no, they do remain true to our recollections. The chance to see what strange creatures and objects were housed in the small pools and to play God as to their destiny.

Well, imagine if you can, the nostalgia of your youth and the lives of the rockpool dwellers and you'll be well-placed to picture this tale of yearning and the sea.

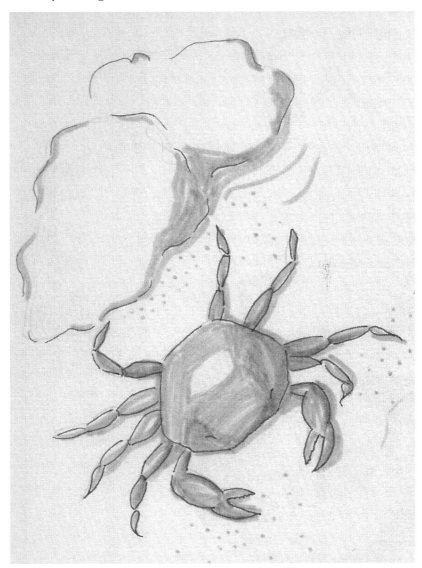

Picture the rockpool and its two most prominent protagonists, one a simple prawn by the name of Peter and his brother-in-arms (well legs, actually) Christian, the crab. Two closer crustaceans you could not find. The pool was theirs, if not alone, but to all intents and purposes they held sway and looked over its realm while sharing their thoughts, fears and dreams. The latter, it must be said, was not so prominent with Christian as with Peter, the former being more pragmatic and feet-on-the-ground (well, claws, actually... enough of such interjections). Peter, however, was a dreamer, harbouring romantic notions of life beyond the salt-watered kingdom.

He didn't shy away when the waters were disturbed by a curious finger, causing ripples in its owner's quest to discover the mysteries that lay beneath the surface. And so it was that both looked on each other's world, deriving knowledge and experience which was destined to ride with the ripples, to the distant shore, never to return nor to unload its secrets.

Looking back, which for a crab is mighty difficult to do, Christian would be hard-pressed not to concede that the morning Peter dropped his bombshell should not have been that much of a surprise. It really shouldn't. But, the fact remained it caught Christian on the hop (well.... no, enough!)

"Oh I wish I'd been a boy," Peter spoke aloud, wearing the face of one who was unaware that he had let his musings escape from himself. "Pardon?!" exclaimed his close friend who, even at the best of times (and this, clearly, was not about to be a time which could in any shape or form fit into that category) would be inclined to take such comments personally. Peter hastily sought to reaffirm his undying friendship with the crab next to him but felt that he now had no option but to articulate his deep desire to be 'of the other world'; to be the one looking down and wiggling his finger in their world. Of course, the conundrum of it no longer being partly his world somewhat of a philosophical torment.

However, he consoled himself with the realisation that, were he to become a boy, he would surely bring with him the knowledge of his days dwelling in the (not so) deep. He would truly be omniscient. Not bad for a prawn; indeed, no mean feat for a boy either.

"Oh Christian, don't you long to find out what's happening up there? How many times have I looked up, willing myself to swap places with those who come to seek out our world. They look so happy, full of curiosity and excitement. They look so, so…." And he searched for the word which would do full justice to what he was feeling, before settling upon, "alive."

Christian pushed aside his bruised feelings, for he could see the yearning on his friend's face and, whilst he didn't remotely share this feeling of wanderlust, he didn't want to see his friend suffer and look so despondent.

"Well, if you really want to be a boy, there's only one thing for it," Christian declared. "The Magic Cove!"

This drew a blank look from Peter. Christian could hardly believe that the topic of the Magic Cove had never come up in their conversation before. True, he was a good couple of years older than Peter and possessed a worldly wisdom which almost transcended the boundaries of the rockpool. He had to explain himself. "The Magic Cove is the answer to everyone's dreams. It lies a long way from home and the journey will be fraught with danger. You must travel through uncountable rockpools until you reach the end of the sands (the term 'beach' being unknown by the rockpool dwellers.)

Peter's face fell as he realised exactly the enormity of this undertaking. "Once there," continued Christian, "you will need to

21

skirt around the rocks before entering a large lane. At the very back of this lane is a dark entrance to the Magic Cove. Inside this chamber is an ethereal light and a warmth which radiates from above and below. It is here that you must tread water for one hour, all the time concentrating upon your heartfelt desire. Indeed, it will only improve your chances if you are to cry out 'I want to be a boy!' during your quest, leaving suitable gaps for the mystical powers to reflect upon your request."

In truth, Christian wasn't too sure about the last bit, but he'd got rather caught up in his own narrative. He was sure that it couldn't do any harm, and if it meant that Peter, whose concentration was known to waver on occasions, were to focus that little bit more, well all the better.

Peter weighed up these wise words. The journey he would have to undertake would be perilous, indeed. But the treading water bit, well, for a prawn that would be nothing out of the ordinary. As for the concentration task… no problem, he thought. It is somewhat strange and more than a little ironic that those possessed of less-than-the-average powers of concentration are always those who believe their forte to be focusing.

"I'm going to do it!" he cried out. Upon hearing these words, Christian involuntarily shook his head (another startling feat for a crab) and at once realised that his relating the existence of the Magic Cove, its whereabouts and how one could harness its powers, had actually been undertaken to scare and dissuade Peter. It had achieved precisely the opposite!

"Listen, Christian. This could be great for both of us," Peter could see his friend was hurt and worried and did not want to exclude him from this adventure. "I'll come to our pool every day and talk with you. We'll know what life is like 'out there'."

At these words, both crab and prawn cast their eyes upwards, looking through the water above as if it were a window through which they could see forever.

And so it was that the following morning, Peter bade Christian an emotional farewell. He would be back, he said. All would be well. He had to do this. Christian nodded (yes, I know you know how difficult this is for a crab) his understanding and wished him every good fortune. In his heart he believed he was saying a final goodbye; he did not expect to see Peter again. Every fibre of his pragmatic body did not believe in the Magic Cove; he was already experiencing guilt at what he saw as being the inevitable death of his dear, dear friend.

Peter's long swim to the Magic Cove isn't recorded and I'm not one to employ poetic licence without good reason. It can, however, be clearly pictured the strenuous efforts he engaged in to ensure his journey was a successful one. It is believed that he travelled over half a mile, passing through countless rockpools at the mercy of the ebb and flow of the tide. Waiting, not so patiently, when the water had receded affording him no further passage. Yes, his determination and will to succeed was, well, I would say superhuman but that would be getting ahead of ourselves in respect of his quest and destiny.

What the story handed down over the years does tell us is that it was a full 10 days from the morning he bade a tearful 'au revoir' to Christian that Peter finally found the 'large lane' of his friend's narration. It certainly lived up to its name and as Peter entered, not without a little trepidation, he found the light receding until it was all but extinguished. He recalled the advice to skirt around the rocks and, hardly choosing to act upon it, doing so as a kind of necessity, being blind to his surroundings. Peter actually possessed a very good recall of Christian's tale and believed him to be the master of understatement when he had talked of a 'dark entrance' to a chamber. "I can't see if it's dark or not," he said to himself, only partly realising the humour in what he had uttered, so intent was he in groping his way forward. To start with, he didn't truly realise that there was a glow ahead. He had been swimming in the dark for so long that the strange light seemed more a hallucination, a figment of his fevered imagination. However, ever so slowly, the passageway became discernible, illuminated by gentle and welcoming glows of a myriad colours, turning his final few yards into that of a kaleidoscope lending a surreal and bewitching feeling to the cove. The light reflected off the water and bounced back from a rock ceiling, seemingly tiled in a 'mother of pearl'. He was drifting now, being lulled into a sense of wonder and calm that had enveloped his whole body. But at the very moment when tragedy appeared to be the outcome of his quest, with Peter falling victim to the visual sirens of the cove, the very enchanting lights began to throb and flash, sending coloured light and shooting stars across the secluded bay.

Peter woke from his reverie and, recalling his task, began to concentrate his mind in a way he had never done before. "I want to be a boy!" This was his mantra as he trod the water in the cove. Indeed, whilst he had the pain of the journey in his body, the water itself was so quiet and still that it aided him in his endeavours. Peter's mind and body were as one, their union allowing a total focus in an almost 'zen-like' state. He was only aroused from his meditative state as he became aware of explosions of light, now accompanied by sound and a very, very strange sensation in his

24

body....

His legs ached; his arms were like lead, at which point he began to sink and was inadvertently gargling the brine of the pool.

The realisation and excitement that he was now, indeed, a boy was only tempered by the knowledge that his newfound existence was almost certainly going to be a very short-lived one. He was drowning! Peter the boy was not the natural water baby he had previously been. It was purely by chance that he found himself at the edge of the cove, the base of which shelved out into the pool allowing Peter's feet to reach the bottom. He was saved.

After sleeping at the side of the cove, Peter swam out – it would seem that he hadn't lost the ability to swim and that it had been the shock of his transformation which had rendered him unable to float the previous evening. Whilst the 'large cove' was sizeable, it was negotiated in fewer than 20 strokes of an enviably graceful front crawl. The light was such that it required Peter to shield his eyes and it was a full 10 minutes before he dared to move, blinking regularly onto the golden sand.

Peter was a boy, seemingly of eight or nine years of age, clad in navy swimming shorts and wearing a rather expensive, waterproof watch. This was, indeed, strange. Stranger still seemed to be the sudden appearance of what he needed, almost as soon as the thought had entered his head. Food, drink, clothes… all appeared. He wanted for nothing.

His new life was to begin and he felt happy… no deliriously happy. He could taste ice cream, fish and chips; he could drink a cooling lemonade. He could use a bucket and spade; he could play and make friends. His old life quickly began to recede from his thoughts… as did his friend, Christian.

It wasn't until a full week after his new life began that, whilst playing with new friends, he found himself looking into a rockpool. All of a sudden, the memory was back with him... and his promise to return to regale Christian with tales of life 'on the other side'. Peter was mortified; tearful, though doing his best to hide it, and humiliated he made hasty excuses and ran along the water's edge. Which was 'his' pool? How would he ever find his once secure and well-loved home?

Indeed, it took a full three days of searching; crouching down by a seemingly endless succession of rockpools desperate to see the familiar frame of his friend. Some pools he could quickly dismiss; too large or too small; too deep or too shallow. But, at last, and with a cry of joy which would have caught the attention of anyone close by (and frustratingly there was no-one), he recognised the pool which had been 'home' for so long. On the far side, curled up against a rise in the sand, nestled Christian.

"Dear Christian!" Peter half thought, half articulated. He placed his right hand into the cool water and moved it back and forth, quite gently as he remembered, all too well, the disturbance and distress endured thanks to the over-exuberant hands and fingers that had disturbed his peace in the past.

Christian opened one eye, looked startled and tried, unsuccessfully, to back away. But looking closer, something made him stop. Peter was now waving and talking animatedly, beaming widely. Christian could hear and understand and, when at last Peter paused for breath, Christian managed a brief greeting.

"Ah. Morning stranger, nice you've found the time to see me," he delivered in a rather icy tone, betraying his sense of bitterness.

Peter had enough sense not to mention his forgetfulness, choosing instead to blame the gap of time as his inability to find the pool. Such was their friendship that, despite his intention to appear otherwise, Christian quickly accepted what he had been told and they fell to talking about Peter's newfound human status. To be truthful, it was, inevitably, Peter who did the greater share of the talking as, of course, it was he who had undergone the transformation. He regaled Christian with tales of the fun he had and was continuing to have.

Beach cricket – the rules of which he was still trying to comprehend so the finer points of the game left Christian none-the-wiser. The culinary delights of the many flavours of ice-cream, triple chocolate being his favourite. Donkey rides… this particular pastime did leave Christian totally bemused, having never seen such a beast in his, comparatively, long life. As Peter continued, both friends began to realise that the physical differences and distances had also made them 'less close.' Christian wasn't jealous; he simply didn't possess the 'free spirit' side which was such a large part of Peter's character. Indeed, when they parted, whilst now agreeing to a morning meeting every day, both reflected upon the change which had occurred. And it was the change in what connected them that dominated both of their minds.

Nevertheless, their friendship remained and, to Peter's great credit, he stayed true to his one and only friend over the following weeks as summer passed in a heat haze. Peter made new friends, but he remained loyal to Christian. For his part, Christian concealed the frustration he sometimes felt as Peter spoke of new excitements and different friends.

However, it was as he left the pool one morning that something was nagging at Peter. He knew what it was; 'new friends'. No sooner had they been made, then they were gone. These friends were transient, staying just as long as their holiday permitted. And it was this 'holiday' that, at first, confirmed and then alarmed Peter. He began to learn of school and work and… 'growing up'. In truth, the latter would still be many years hence but the first of this worrying triumvirate left Peter very cold and this had nothing to do with the stiffening breeze which now accompanied the still bright late August days. Peter thought. And the more he thought, the less he played. On more than one occasion he went a whole day without experiencing ice cream....

And so it fell that, one day, he found himself opening up to Christian. "I'm not sure I want to be a boy anymore. I'm going to lose my friends and I'll no longer have the happy days, playing and having no cares," he wailed. "I want to come back." He lowered his face as the tears began to fall, bouncing off the surface of the pool.

Christian, who had suspected that this day may come around,

felt for his friend and did his best to conceal his excitement and joy at the return of the prodigal boy. "Well, if you're sure, you know what you need to do," he counselled. "It won't take you any time to get there, but treading the water for an hour is going to be a whole new proposition."

Peter wiped away a last, lingering tear. He nodded his thanks and, with a brief smile, turned and left.

He determined that he needed to go back to the Magic Cove and he headed there, with a steadily increasing sense of purpose in his footfall. The Cove loomed before him, but he swept through the water, swam and then floated into the dark before meeting the beguiling lights of the Magic Cove.

Once in, he wasted no time; he closed his eyes, concentrated and tried not to tense his muscles whilst focusing his thoughts.

Time seemed to pass slowly. Peter remained steadfast, yet his body began to scream. Every fibre was aching and certain muscles were burning. As he neared the conclusion of his quest, Peter fought against the pull of the water. His mouth filled with the salty water and he gargled and spat as the brine brought him back from the brink. Just as he could last no longer, lights flashed and canons sounded... and Peter floated on the surface. He was as light as the air.

Peter found himself at the Cove's edge after a full 12 hours had passed. Whilst this unscheduled and unexpected sleep had refreshed his body somewhat, he remained exhausted. With a smile of contentment, he closed his eyes once more and slipped back, wrapped in the blanket of dreams.

Christian was busying himself which, given that he had no one else to talk to and precious little to do, was not all that easy to achieve. It was, therefore, with more than a degree of alarm that he suddenly became aware of a foreign body in his dwelling place. On closer inspection, he realised that this was no interloper, but none other than Peter. He was overjoyed and could not conceal his happiness.

For his part, Peter looked possibly even more content. He beamed, exuding how he felt about his return.

"Oh Peter. Is it really you?" cried Christian.

"It is," was all Peter could reply, frantically nodding as a means to make up for his lack of words.

"You've come back. You look so happy. But what about your new friends?" enquired the crab.

"It was a treat, but it wasn't really me," Peter tried to explain.

"But the games, the ice cream, the new friends…" his true friend's voice trailed off as emotion overcame him. He recovered and continued. "You just look so happy?" His statement, perhaps betraying his lack of certainty at his friend's return, came out as a question. Realising this, he chose to underline it in the solitary word, "Why?"

Peter looked him straight in the eyes and, with a beaming face, replied. "It's simple. I'm a prawn again, Christian."

THE BLOODY RED KNIGHT ON
THE BLOODY RED HORSE

In a land far, far away and at a time even further away from today, there existed a Knight so fabled and renowned that his aura and mystique spread across the known world. True, the known world, it is known, was nowhere near the known world we know today.

That said, the Bloody Red Knight was, and remains, a legendary figure. His bravery, hand-to-hand combat and swordsmanship drew comparison to NO other warrior, living or deceased. To this, he was an inspirational leader who gained the respect and love of all over whom he had charge and those who had the misfortune to be opposed to him or his cause. And he was chivalrous, a Knight who exuded gentileese; a man whose nobility was peerless. I say 'was' but I am getting ahead of myself. 'Is', most definitely 'is'.

Let me explain why the short confusion with the tense. Or rather, let me let the heroic figure speak for himself and you will understand as his story unfolds.

There was nothing more to be done, he concluded. He had to speak to the King. His Majesty would grant him an audience, of that he had no doubt whatsoever.

This wasn't monumental arrogance or folly on his part; no, it simply reflected the very close relationship the two shared. The King had good reason to have such a bond with his kinsman as many a time he had defended the Kingdom from the numerous threats which seemed ever present.

He left his castle and mounted his trusty steed; the Bloody Red Horse, itself a warrior of great repute. They shared a mutual love and respect which transferred to what might be termed 'an intuition.' Their movement and actions complemented one another and appeared so seamless as to say to any observer 'We are one.' Brave, resolute and fearless, this did not prevent each displaying their clear affection for each other. With a gentle pat of spurs from his right ankle, they departed.

It was only the swiftest of journeys as the Bloody Red Knight was, in effect, the monarch's neighbour. No sooner had the piebald stallion begun to streak through the rural pastures, than the walled ramparts of the King's castle came into sight. Easing to a canter and then a stately trot, befitting his stature, he approached the gatehouse and knocked upon the door. A rapping noise something like this: one long, two short and a final long rap.

A rather timid and, it seemed, slightly bored voice responded from within. "Yes, who goes there?"

'The Bloody Red Knight on the Bloody Red Horse," came the rather abrupt reply. The tone within the gatehouse changed immediately.

"Not, not THE Bloody Red Knight," stammered the guard.

"Yes, THE Bloody Red Knight," he repeated.

"Well, you better come in then."

The bolts and levers were moved and the various security devices disabled to allow the Bloody Red Knight on the Bloody Red Horse to enter. They passed through and every man, woman and child who was safely ensconced within the castle walls, stopped and stared.

They were held in awe, a silence descended and time seemed to slow in deference as both warrior and steed made their stately procession towards the King's chambers.

The Bloody Red Knight dismounted his faithful friend and stood at the door to his monarch's private dwelling. He summoned his courage, which was, in itself, an unusual action as courage oozed from his every pore. But today he was nervous.

Not from greeting the great King, as he had enjoyed many a private audience. No, it was what he had to request that was making him feel.... fear.

He had to be bold and resolute. No turning back. He was, after all, the Bloody Red Knight. As this moment of self-reflection seemed to instil the necessary self-belief, he rapped upon the King's chambers' door, something like this. One long, two short and a final long rap.

"Yes, who is it?" The tone of the monarch suggested he was already engaged and this would, without a shadow of a doubt, lessen the resolve of anyone other than the Bloody Red Knight.

"It is the Bloody Red Knight, sire!" he duly responded, although anyone listening very attentively may have been aware of a slight tremor to his voice on his annunciation of the word, 'Sire'.

This seeming hint of self-doubt was banished immediately on hearing the joyful response of his Monarch.

"Not, THE Bloody Red Knight?!" apparently unable to contain his pleasure at receiving such a visitor.

"Yes, THE Bloody Red Knight," replied the aforementioned Bloody Red Knight, with confidence returning to him as he confirmed his identify.

"Well, come on in, come on in," cried the delighted monarch.

On greeting the Bloody Red Knight, the King showered him with questions as to his welfare and how he had been keeping. In truth, their conversation proceeded such for a good while with both sharing stories of how their lives had been since their last meeting. We have no need to go into this detail; indeed, much of it was private and it would paint me in a very poor light were I to reveal such intimacies. No, it must remain with them; I cannot allow any distractions to delay me from relaying the tale I set out to tell.

Let it never be said that I wander from my ambition; and, in so saying, I wish to make it clear that what is about to be requested and what then ensues is the story I tell to you. Nothing more. Nothing may allow me to digress.

I return to the King's chambers....

At a seemingly appropriate and convenient pause in their reflections, the Bloody Red Knight cleared his throat, summoned his resolve and ventured his request.

"My Lord," further deference, he deemed, being an important way to approach the topic in hand.

"My Lord," he repeated, perhaps betraying an underlying trepidation? "I wish to be as bold as to venture a personal request." No sooner had those words left his lips then the King interjected enthusiastically. "Say it, name it and it will be yours, fearless and faithful friend." It should be noted that the King had recently been reading the adventure of Sir Gawain in his quests with the Green Knight, and the alliterative verses seemed to have emerged, on occasion, in his everyday speech. His reading material was, as you will read, very apt.

The Bloody Red Knight's face fell a little. Not because of the willingness to grant him anything he desired on the part of the King, his friend. Oh no, it was because of what he was about to request. "My Lord," again he assumed the deference of formality. "I have fought for you and our great Kingdom for over 40 years. I remain totally devoted; yet also remain... alone." At this his voice failed, before he gathered his courage and, with full feeling and fervour (having seemingly caught the alliterative manner of his monarch), continued. "I am looking for a wife. I wish to have a partner and be happy…. And I come to ask of you the hand of your fair daughter, Isobel."

There. He had done it. He had said it. He dared to glance up and now it was the turn of the King's face to have fallen a little.

"Oh my brave Bloody Red Knight," he began. His tone seemed not to augur well. "If only it were so easy. You would be the perfect son-in-law, but you don't know what you'll be letting yourself in for."

A silence fell within the room, it rested there for what seemed more time than was really the case as both the King and the Bloody Red Knight were slowly shaking their lowered heads as they gazed, as if in some despondent dream, at the soft white fur rug which carpeted that particular section of the stone-flagged floor.

"But what am I thinking?!" cried the King, all of a sudden. His returning joy and enthusiasm dispelling the silence which hastily removed itself from their presence. "You are the Bloody Red Knight."

"Indeed, I am," thought our eponymous hero, but before he could allow his thoughts to form into spoken words, the King continued.

"You will succeed. You have always succeeded. You shall, I know, win the hand of my beloved daughter." And at this point, he lowered his voice to little more than a conspiratorial whisper, "And I know that she thinks of you so highly. To know that you would be her suitor would be beyond her wildest dreams."

And before he could reply, he summoned his daughter, informed her of his friend's desire and waited for her response.

In truth, the Bloody Red Knight wouldn't have chosen this to be the way his heart's desire was revealed to his intended but in a modern day parlance, had the turn of events been unfolding in contemporary days, 'It was what it was' or 'was what it is' or, most likely, and just as confusingly, in a temporal scheme of things, 'it is what it was.'

He smiled at Isobel for, despite his great bravery, he remained nervous. This was a quest he had never experienced before.

His nerves were quickly cast aside as the beautiful and articulate Isobel expressed that she had dreamed of this day and could scarcely wait for their engagement to be announced to the Kingdom. It would, she assured him, bring joy and happiness to all.

"Quite so, quite so" agreed the King, her father. "However, my dearest," he continued. "You are aware that any suitor wishing to marry into the royal lineage must perform three acts of unparalleled daring and heroism, just as I had to do to win the heart of your dear, sweet, late mother. A tear entered the octogenarian's eye, noted by both in his audience. He had been a widower for more than 15 years and he, himself, had been the bravest of warriors in his day. The loss of his queen still sat very heavily upon him and the thought of his valiant friend undertaking life-threatening quests filled him with dismay. And yet he would not have felt more pride than if he were to welcome the Bloody Red Knight into his family and satisfy the longing of his only child, his beloved Isobel.

Custom had it, although in truth the King could only draw upon his experience as being 'the custom', that what lay ahead of the suitor could only be heard by him from the monarch. Lady Isobel politely and gracefully took her leave, but not before planting a loving kiss upon the cheek of the Bloody Red Knight. He clasped both of her hands in his as he did so and would fain have not let go should he have had the chance so to do. However, the knowledge that the sooner they parted then the sooner they would be reunited allowed him, with reluctance, to release her hands and watch as she floated out of the chamber.

The King turned to his friend and despite what he was to reveal, smiling began to explain the wretched and ruinous road that had to be ridden before he would be a member of the royal family. Before he continued, he sat back and, inwardly, congratulated himself on his growing narrative prowess. Shaking himself from his reverie, he looked his friend in the eye. Well, actually, in both eyes and began.

"To marry Isobel and become a member of the royal family, you need to successfully complete," at this the Bloody Red Knight winced slightly. It was not at the thought of what he would need to successfully complete, but at such a flagrant splitting of the infinitive. The King's alliterative acumen was to be acknowledged, but one of the more complex syntactical rules he had wilfully trounced.

"Let it be," thought his friend and returned to the role of attentive listener.

It would appear that the King had not proceeded much further for the Bloody Red Knight swiftly ascertained that he needed to complete three perilous quests which would bring him (even greater) fame and honour, whilst also showering prestige upon the Kingdom.

"Sire," uttered the Bloody Red Knight. "Your wish is but my

command. Let me know the first quest."

"Indeed, it may be only the first quest that I can reveal. Not, I hasten to add, because I fear you will fail to accomplish it. On no, but purely because this is the rule handed down to me. I was bequeathed the procedure and must remain true to it."

"I would wish it no other way, my liege and lord," the Bloody Red Knight humbly replied.

"You are to bring back the Etruscan Diamond from the neighbouring kingdom of Arrowata. You know only too well how much these are our sworn enemies. I would far rather you had a different goal and a rendezvous with a different people, but the choice is not mine. It is said the diamond is three feet tall and two feet wide. It is reputed to be surprisingly light, which may be of assistance to you. It is flawless, casting beautiful pictures and shadows as the light catches its gleaming contours. It is priceless. It is beyond compare."

The Bloody Red Knight drew in his cheeks in a deep inward breath. This was, indeed a perilous task he had been given. He had fought against the Arrowatan people on many occasions over the past 40 years; he would hardly be a welcome visitor!

But this was the quest. Having heard it and appreciating its enormity, the Bloody Red Knight rose and took his leave, adding to his friend, that he would soon return with the Etruscan Diamond.

"Fare you well, my faithful friend. God's speed be with you and your noble steed," the King offered as his final words, inwardly fearing, yet hoping against such fears, that these may be the last words he uttered to his companion.

A reflective Bloody Red Knight mounted the Bloody Red Horse, who had been waiting so patiently for his master's return. He trotted back to the gatehouse door and the Bloody Red Knight knocked upon it, something like this one long, two short and a final long rap.

"Halt, who goes there?" enquired the sentry.

"It's the Bloody Red Knight on the Bloody Red Horse," replied our hero.

"Not THE Bloody Red Knight on the Bloody Red Horse?" responded the sentry.

"Yes, THE Bloody Red Knight on the Bloody Red Horse," he rejoined.

"Well, I'll let you both out then." which he duly did.

Time passed, but our hero's resolve only stiffened. He planned meticulously and a mere six weeks later he found himself, secreted, very close to the Tower of Belax, inside of which there was a room which housed the Etruscan Diamond. I would love to be able to relate to you just how he succeeded in getting this far, but these details were spared me for the route is so secret and precious its revelation would bring vulnerability to the Bloody Red Knight's kingdom. Suffice for me to say that the journey was arduous and he had to leave his faithful steed hidden and secure a mile away from where he was standing.

He had spent many, many nights studying his astrological charts. Indeed, a strong knowledge of such was the staple of any good knight. He, however, was the Bloody Red Knight; his knowledge was without compare. He knew that on this very night if he, the knight, found himself with the sky clear, which it was, the light from the Northern Star would offer a shaft of protection into which he could slip and under cover of its glare (ironically, thanks to the reflections of the Etruscan Diamond) he would have three and half minutes to spirit away the beauty.

He was more stealthy than stealth itself. His imposing figure seemed to melt into the surroundings as he swept to the diamond. He had schooled himself not to be entranced by its beauty and it was only due to his meticulous pragmatism that he did not feel bewitched by its majesty.

No sooner had he held the famed jewel in his hands, and he was gone. The role of thief didn't sit comfortably with him, but the danger of the quest and the richness of his reward were enough to banish such a moral dilemma from his consciousness. He became air and light and was into full flight, a quarter of a mile distant from the Tower of Belax before the mythical protection of the Northern Star lost its lustre. He sailed forth, under cover of the wooded enclave, but had not made more than 100 yards before he heard a desperate wailing sound. Filled with determination and quickened by the knowledge of the fate that would befall him should he be caught, he sped to meet his faithful steed.

As he approached the Bloody Red Horse, the very night seemed to rip and a thunderous chorus bellowed its fury as the beating of hooves filled the air. Our intrepid duo fled the area as fast as was possible.

Fortune favoured them as their route back into their kingdom, the closely guarded secret, lay no more than an hour's hard and punishing ride. It was touch and go. Had the entrance been more than a minute's gallop further, then my tale could have ended and the beautiful Lady Isobel's heart would have been broken.

The Bloody Red Horse leapt into a seeming abyss… only to be taken, riding on a seeming slipstream and swept into the serenity of safety. Both horse and its mount could scarcely breathe and yet each looked at the other, quizzically, on the realisation that the king's alliterative bent had been more far reaching than either had recognised.

In Arrowata, the nation subsided into a state of baleful mourning. The woeful cries of the tormented souls made the pitiful moaning of the sirens seem but the voiced tantrum of a petulant child. But their loss and grief is not my tale. I will tell of the Bloody Red Knight and the Bloody Red Horse who, exhausted, once safe and secure, made their way to the gatehouse of the Royal Palace.

The Bloody Red Knight knocked on the gatehouse door,

something like this: one long, two short and a final long rap.

"Halt, who goes there?" enquired the voice from within.

"It's the Bloody Red Knight on the Bloody Red Horse with the Etruscan Diamond," replied our hero.

"Not THE Bloody Red Knight on the Bloody Red Horse with the Etruscan Diamond?" responded the sentry.

"Yes, THE Bloody Red Knight on the Bloody Red Horse with the Etruscan Diamond," he replied.

"Well, you must come in."

Our fearless duo approached the King's chamber's door and, dismounting, the Bloody Red Knight knocked respectfully upon the door, something like this: one long, two short and a final long rap.

"Who is it?" inquired the King.

"It's the Bloody Red Knight and the Bloody Red Horse with the Etruscan Diamond, Sire."

"Not THE Bloody Red Knight on the Bloody Red Horse with the Etruscan Diamond?" spluttered a clearly overjoyed monarch.

"Yes, THE Bloody Red Knight on the Bloody Red Horse with the Etruscan Diamond," replied the Bloody Red Knight.

"Well come in, come in. Let me greet you."

The King was, indeed, so overjoyed at seeing his friend again that he flung his arms around him in an action most unroyal. But it was one which told of true love and friendship.

The Bloody Red Knight brought forth the Etruscan Diamond. He handed it to his monarch and they both stared, mesmerised by its beauty. But before they were truly bewitched by it, the King took it to a very well hidden room in his chamber. The door to this room was cunningly disguised as part of a mural. Only he, and now his friend (and you, esteemed reader), knew of its existence.

"The Etruscan Diamond must reside there, safe, until it is needed at the end of your quest," he pronounced.

"And that, my Lord, is my most pressing thought. I beg to know the nature of my second adventure. I yearn its completion as I so desire my betrothal to the fair Isobel," said the Bloody Red Knight.

"Yes, of course. We must move swiftly. One quest is achieved, the next awaits. And this will take you on a long, long journey to the ends of the very known world. It is here, in the Forest of Despair that you must retrieve the mystical Golden Fleece. Once claimed by Jason, but now lost to the clutches of our deepest and darkest dreams, in a place from which no-one is known to have returned."

As soon as the king had uttered that final sentence, he wished that he had not. But, too late. What has been said cannot be unsaid.

The Bloody Red Knight smiled, politely, in return. He was all too aware of the myths and stories which surrounded the Forest of Despair. His enemy would not be a fearsome external presence, he pondered, but the further fathoms of his own id. The quest pitched him against himself. The question to be answered was whether he could return valiant and unvanquished.

Declining all offers to dine that evening at the Palace, the Bloody Red Knight took his leave and, upon exiting the King's chambers, his mind immediately turned to his new quest. He approached the

Gatehouse door and, deep in thought, rapped upon it, something like this. One long, two short and a final long rap.

"Please, who goes there," enquired a rather polite gatekeeper.

"It's the Bloody Red Knight on the Bloody Red Horse."

"Not THE Bloody Red Knight on the Bloody Red Horse?"

"Yes, THE Bloody Red Knight on the Bloody Red Horse," he replied crisply.

"Well please leave and God be with you," ventured the Gatekeeper, his life so much the richer having both seen and conversed with such a Herculean figure.

It is at this point that I must confess there is little documented as to how the Bloody Red Knight arrived at the 'end of the known world'. It has already been established that what was then 'the known world' was not, in all truth, all that much to know. Yes, today's greater powers of access and speed of communication would appear to dwarf such little knowledge. But lest we become too self-congratulatory, we would do well to remember that the land then known was full of peril and could not be travelled without taking a great risk.

It must be assumed that on arriving at the Forest of Despair, our brave pair was completely fatigued and in need of rest and recuperation before entering the Woebegone Woodland of Weir whose tangled trees tormented, terrorised and terrified all travellers. The range of the alliterative semantic field was clearly growing and would pose an added and heavy burden as they were to make their way towards their destination.

A full three days passed before they could summon the strength to enter the dark and forbidding forest. The very foliage snatched at their limbs and sapped them of their energy. The vines twisted and turned upon them, whispering as serpents, convincing them of their own lack of worth whilst trying to turn rider and steed against one another.

But they were prepared. The Bloody Red Knight's flashing sword sliced swathes through the stems which surrounded them.

Agonised cries rendered the air and the darkness deepened as it sought to spread its gloom and despondency. At their very lowest point, when all seemed lost, a flickering, golden hue in the near distance revealed itself and acted as a beacon which spurred on the Bloody Red Knight and Bloody Red Horse.

Much like a mirage, the golden light flickered, in and out of focus, never seeming to get closer. Yet there it remained, tantalising, their only hope. And just when all seemed lost, its shape began to grow. The Bloody Red Knight was conscious of a slight warmth and as he and his faithful steed moved ever onward, the warmth grew. It reached out to them and seemingly wrapped itself around them giving comfort and restoring faith. And then, as if in a trance, they broke through what was the last of the gnarled and withered branches.

The glittering fleece hung from a living tree, a source of natural goodness and health amidst such sickness and disease.

The Bloody Red Knight staggered from his mount. As if in a fevered dream, he reached up and gathered down the beautiful blanket. His very first thought was for his horse which, collapsed on the ground, saw his intention with grateful eyes. He wrapped it around the stallion's body and stroked his mane. New life and vigour returned to the magnificent beast almost instantaneously. But not until he was sure that his partner was fully restored did he slip the blanket around his own shoulders. He lay resting his head upon the warm flank of the Bloody Red Horse. Strength and vitality began to course through his veins and within a few moments more he was, once again, the very embodiment of the valiant warrior who had begun the quest.

Restored and sharing the fleece between them, their exit from the Forest of Despair was swift. Indeed, I can reveal the path they took saw new life grow from every step taken by the Bloody Red Horse. A path of hope and positivity emerged from the dark devastation. The forest would be changed.... Forever.

The journey back to the home kingdom was still a long one, but it was one they undertook with joy and triumph. As they approached the familiar gatehouse door, the Bloody Red Knight allowed himself a very quiet little chuckle, as if to say, 'I'm home'.

It was with vigour that he rapped upon the gatehouse door, something like this: one long, two short and a final long rap.

"Halt, who goes there?" was the seemingly instant reply.

"It's the Bloody Red Knight on the Bloody Red Horse with the Golden Fleece", he countered.

"Not THE Bloody Red Knight on the Bloody Red Horse with the Golden Fleece?" came the incredulous reply.

"Yes, THE Bloody Red Knight on the Bloody Red Horse with the Golden Fleece," repeated our hero.

"Oh please, please come in." And with that, the gate was flung open and the warrior and his steed trotted slowly yet purposefully and respectfully towards the King's chamber. Arriving at the door, the Bloody Red Knight announced his return with a familiar knock on the wood: one long, two short and a final long rap.

"Who is it blease?" enquired the monarch, for it appeared he was suffering with a heavy cold.

"It's the Bloody Red Knight on the Bloody Red Horse with the Golden Fleece," announced the joyful warrior.

"Not de Bloody Red Knight on de Bloody Red Horse wid de Golden Fleece?" replied his king, scarcely believing his own ears.

"Yes, THE Bloody Red Knight on the Bloody Red Horse with the Golden Fleece."

"Come in, come in, come IN my faithful, fearledd friend." His blocked sinuses still making normal speech a very tricky proposition.

Immediately upon entering the room, the Bloody Red Knight put the Golden Fleece around the king. His cold disappeared; he was the picture of rude health.

"You are a truly magnificent servant to the kingdom, my friend.

You have achieved what no mortal has ever done. You have returned from the Forest of Despair. The Golden Fleece will protect our great kingdom and bring health and prosperity to all. I salute you."

Somewhat abashed, as he remained the modest and unassuming knight he always had been, the Bloody Red Knight smiled graciously in recognition of the words of praise which had been lavished upon him. He bowed his head and spoke quietly.

"I ask only to serve you, my Lord. And in so saying, I humbly request to hear of my third and final quest. I feel close to the dear Isobel and wish with all my heart to complete the trilogy of treacherous tasks that test me."

He stopped at this point, taken aback by his own alliterative prose. His articulation was not lost on his host whose admiration, were it possible, which it wasn't, could only have grown.

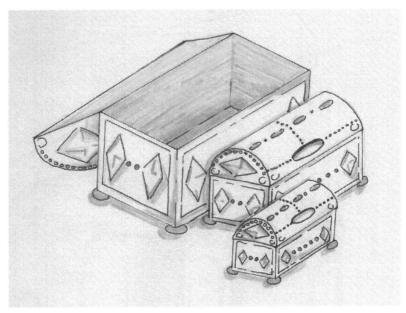

"Your final quest brave Knight is to bring back the fabled jewelled boxes from the kingdom of Scarota. These jewelled treasures are rightfully ours, but were stolen from our kingdom during the Sixty Year War, some two generations ago. There are seven boxes, all identically jewelled, each very slightly smaller than its predecessor allowing each to fit inside the other in a manner which is tight and comfortable." The king may have made the comparison to Russian Dolls had he or any in his kingdom been aware of their existence.

They weren't. So he didn't.

The Bloody Red Knight was aware of the existence of the seven jewelled boxes; their fabled beauty and craftsmanship was said to be unparalleled. Jewels of every colour; jewels which were no longer seen. This was, indeed, a very fitting final quest.

Once more he declined supper, leaving only after the King had secreted the Golden Fleece behind the hidden door of the mural. He took his leave in the most gentle and polite manner and it was with such humility that he knocked upon the gatehouse door to secure his exit, something like this: One long, two short and a final long rap.

"Hello, how can I help you?" was the sincere and genuine call from above.

"It's the Bloody Red Knight on the Bloody Red Horse," he replied.

"Not THE Bloody Red Knight on the Bloody Red Horse?" came back in astonishment.

"Yes, THE Bloody Red Knight on the Bloody Red Horse," he confirmed.

"Oh please let me open the gateway for you, Sire." And with that both horse and warrior departed.

The seven jewelled boxes would pose a huge challenge of that there could be no question. However, the challenge the quest was to offer was slightly different. Whilst the loss of the seven jewelled boxes occurred at a time of great conflict between the two nations, the Bloody Red Knight was fully aware of the celebrated peace and good relations his own kingdom now shared with the Scarota people. And the seven jewelled boxes, far from being hidden away, were deemed a national treasure and put on public display.

At this point, it should be added, that Scarota also laid claim to the seven jewelled boxes being their own, claiming them to have been stolen two centuries before. Claim and counter claim, the truth is lost in the mists of time. Nevertheless, the fact remained that they were proudly displayed, with a strong security presence, in their current home.

The Bloody Red Knight spent many nights reading accounts of the Sixty Year War. This he did to try to appreciate the strength of feeling that had set two great kingdoms at each other's throats. This wise and worldly warrior had his own personal tragedy buried in the annals of history in a more violent time: the loss of both his father and uncle, two great warriors themselves. When young, revenge had burned in him but his age, experience and chivalry had seen him able to douse the flame of fury associated with the most basic emotion of vengeance. He championed greater virtues. And, closing another tome on the troubled past, he determined that he would bring back the seven jewelled boxes but that they would only remain temporarily.

He would return them to Scarota at a later, to be fixed, date.

Hoping this was more than a salve to his conscience, he turned to sleep for a final night before he began his third quest.

As with the preceding quests, his journey to the Scarota Royal Palace is not documented. It is, however, recorded that it took longer than may have been expected for what was, in truth, a twelfth of the distance he and his brave stallion travelled to the Forest of Despair. Why this was, no-one knows. All that has been relayed to us begins when he is inside the Palace walls, the Bloody Red Horse safely stowed in a luscious pasture adjacent to the road which arrived at the formidable royal lodgings. He had forsaken his full armour, relying more on wit, tactics and prayer. On the surface, these three appeared insufficient and yet, as we are aware, faith can move mountains. This faith found him in a more remote guard house, in which he was able to don the apparel of the Scarota guard. By so doing, he became one of many within the Palace walls and was able to move around with relative freedom. In this he was more fortunate as he had donned the uniform of a Chief of Guards whose words and actions would be beyond question. I say it was fortune, but perhaps this was destiny working? A quest based on the very foundations and strength of true love deserved and cried out for its success.

The crowds began to dispel. The guards looked to him for their orders and duties. At twilight he was left alone in the ante room which housed the seven jewelled boxes. Their beauty was, indeed, rare. The precious stones shone and glinted, reflecting colours of all hues, and some which time has now forgotten. Enthralled by such splendour and, as if in a dream, he picked up the largest box, which contained all of its smaller siblings, and walked from the room. Quite how he was unseen, or if that were the case as more than one account of this tale claims that at this very time each

53

evening the boxes were taken to be secured in a safer, more private area, is unclear. Whatever the actual fact, the Bloody Red Knight walked out with the boxes and continued walking, unchallenged. He had thought to take a large bag into which he transferred the boxes at a judicious moment in the proceedings. Almost before he was aware he found himself astride the Bloody Red Horse and with that, they began the return leg of their journey. No word reached him of any alarm at the Scarota Palace and so, largely untroubled it would seem, they arrived back at the Gatehouse which controlled entrances and exits to his own King's Palace.

A rather sprightly Bloody Red Knight rapped upon the door, something like this: One long, two short and a final long rap.

"Halt who goes there?" was the response.

"It's the Bloody Red Knight on the Bloody Red Horse with the seven jewelled boxes," he replied.

"Not THE Bloody Red Knight on the Bloody Red Horse with the seven jewelled boxes?" came the immediate reply.

"Yes, THE Bloody Red Knight on the Bloody Red Horse with the seven jewelled boxes."

"Please come in, oh great warrior."

Both Knight and steed proceeded at a stately pace until they reached the King's chambers. Dismounting, and giving the Bloody Red Horse an affectionate stroke on his nose, the Bloody Red Knight knocked quietly on the chamber door, something like this: one long, two short and a final long rap.

"Hello, who is it please?" came a voice from within.

"It's the Bloody Red Knight on the Bloody Red Horse with the seven jewelled boxes," he replied, controlling the joy in his voice.

"Not THE Bloody Red Knight on the Bloody Red Horse with the seven jewelled boxes?" came the excited voice, not concealing in the slightest the joy from behind the door.

"Yes, THE Bloody Red Knight on the Bloody Red Horse with the seven jewelled boxes" he politely confirmed.

"Oh come in, please come in, my valiant warrior and my son."

The King was truly overjoyed to receive back the Bloody Red Knight for the final time. He listened, enraptured, to the tale the brave knight relayed to him. They then both stared at the boxes, taking each out from the other until seven identical boxes sat side by side. They were, indeed, exquisite in their design and craftsmanship.

The Bloody Red Knight looked at his king, bowed down and upon bended knee made a formal request for his daughter's hand in marriage. The King assented immediately but then conceded that he had to add a final request.

"It does not require you to leave my presence and can be done here and now," he continued. And with this he drew back his silver locks which fell to his shoulder, as was the custom and fashion in his kingdom, to reveal that he had no left ear. It had clearly been sliced from his head and by looking at the scar that remained this had occurred many years before.

The Bloody Red Knight began to speak but his Lord raised his hand to explain.

"As I married into the royal line, this act of self-sacrifice was required of me as it had been of any other in centuries before.

Brave, brave Bloody Red Knight, to access our family and to win my daughter's hand I have to ask you to do likewise. I will stem the blood flow and seal the self-inflicted wound with great care. Indeed, I have thought about this long and hard since you began your third quest and feel the Golden Fleece will aid us both in this action."

The Bloody Red Knight had listened intently as in fairness he always did. If he were being honest which, of course, he always was, he didn't relish slicing off his left ear.

He had become particularly attached to it. And the right one, come to think of it. However, he had gone through so much and his love for the fair Isobel was incomparable, it seemed to consume his very being.

"My Lord, I understand and will fully oblige you."

With that, the King retrieved the Golden Fleece from behind the door within the mural; the Bloody Red Knight pulled back his own flowing locks, which showed a sabling at their ends which offered his dark tresses a slightly glittery effect and he swiftly severed his ear with his sharp dagger held firmly in his right hand. With ear in his left hand, and the Golden Fleece instantly wrapped about his head and shoulders he seemed to feel no pain; nor did he appear to suffer any loss of blood.

He handed the left ear to his king who very carefully, opening the smallest of the seven jewelled boxes and bestowed it safely inside. He then placed each of the boxes inside the next increasing size before all that remained visible was the largest of all the seven wonders.

"And now I will return the Golden Fleece to its secret room and add the seven jewelled boxes. The three treasures you have brought back I will carefully wrap and these will be presents you give to my daughter, your wife, as wedding gifts," he said with great pride and, as was very clear, a similar amount of affection for his future son-in-law.

And so it was that the Bloody Red Knight and the fair Lady Isobel were married. There was great rejoicing throughout the kingdom on the days leading up to the happy event. The guest list for the celebratory banquet was hugely impressive although, unsurprisingly, it didn't feature anyone from Arrowota nor, I believe, from the kingdom of Scarota, whether the latter knew of the whereabouts of the seven jewelled boxes remains unclear.

The day was a tremendous success bringing immense happiness to the couple, the King and all of the people.

As befitted such a modest man, the Bloody Red Knight wished for a very quiet and simple honeymoon at a location in the mountains in a small and modest lodging by a lake. The married couple had a wonderful two weeks in each other's company before returning, unobtrusively, to the royal homestead which would, for the immediate future, be their dwelling place. That night, once the Bloody Red Knight was secure in the knowledge that the Bloody Red Horse was safe and content in his stabled lodging, they returned to their quarters but not before visiting Lady Isobel's father to thank him, once again, for such a splendid wedding.

They ate their first supper as a married couple in their new home. And then returned to their seats in front of a roaring fire in the hearth. Each with a glass of wine, the Bloody Red Knight encouraged his wife to open the wedding presents. There were, as you may well imagine, a great many and they comprised surprises both great and small. People had been truly generous.

Finally, the Bloody Red Knight brought forth three presents, which he handed to his wife.

"My dear," he said, "these gifts are very special and are from me to you as a means of sealing our love and life together." With that, he handed the first gift, which had been carefully wrapped by the good King himself. For its size, it was surprisingly light. Lady Isobel's excitement was very evident as she quickly tore away the paper to reveal the beauty of the Etruscan Diamond. She was speechless as she marvelled its beauty, the light from the fireside being caught and cascaded across carpets and curtains, captivating the couple in alliterative adoration.

"It is the famous Etruscan Diamond, my love," the Bloody Red Knight said in a simple, understated way.

"You brought this for me? You risked your life?" Tears sprang from her eyes as she uttered those words.

Before she could say or do anything more, the Bloody Red Knight handed her his second gift. Soft, warm and comforting, even within the expert wrapping of her father, Lady Isobel quickly revealed The Golden Fleece.

"It is Jason's long lost Golden Fleece which has fabled restorative powers. With this we can bring great goodness and health to all," her husband announced.

Lady Isobel buried her face in its luxurious warmth and felt safe and deliriously happy. She had so much to say; but could not find the words with which to begin.

Before she could, her husband revealed his third and final gift, handing it to her with great care. As if in a dream, she accepted it gratefully before beginning to unwrap the parcel. The comfort of the Golden Fleece had slowed her speed and she now took time and care to peel back the paper before revealing a beautiful jewelled box.

Scarcely able to believe her eyes, she sat and stared at the sublime creation which lay on her lap. "The colours, the jewels, the beauty, the skill, the time…." at which point she broke off, overcome with emotion.

"My dearest love," explained her husband. "These are the seven jewelled boxes – truly a wonder of our known world."

"Seven?!" Lady Isobel repeated in astonishment. And at this she placed the box upon the table which sat between them before the fire. Opening the lid, very carefully, she took another.

"It's so beautiful and just the same as the larger one." Her fair fingers placed it next to the larger one and swiftly she opened the slightly smaller of the two to reveal a third. This was placed alongside the second one and then there were three, in descending order of size, sat next to each other. Lady Isobel stopped, choosing to marvel at what she saw, before opening the lid of the box she had most recently revealed to clasp eyes on a fourth. This box replicated, identical to the preceding three, differing only by being that slight bit smaller.

The light from the Etruscan Diamond and the sheen cast by the Golden Fleece seemed to illuminate the beauty of the many and manifold jewels which bedecked each of the surfaces of each of the boxes.

"Continue my love," urged the Bloody Red Knight. Opening the lid of the fourth box his wife dutifully revealed a fifth. This, too, was as wondrous and captivating as those already on show. Without further thought, Lady Isobel lifted the lid of the fifth box to be met by a sixth, the jewels winking, somewhat conspiratorially at her. Her slender fingers retrieved the box and placed it next to its slightly larger sibling.

"One, two, three, four, five, six..." Lady Isobel turned to her husband who nodded his approval as she opened the lid of the sixth box, only to reveal the seventh. Its beauty was no more than the others, being identical, but perhaps its small size made it seem even more exquisite. Lady Isobel made to place it in line to complete the peerless parade but stopped just as her hand was to meet the table.

She brought the smallest box closer to her. Surely there was something precious inside it? Opening the lid and peering in, she turned to the Bloody Red Knight and gently enquired, "What's this 'ere?"

A LONE SHARK

Sidney the Shark was renowned as a sharp operator. That he was harsh and firm in his dealings was given. Some would call his practices ruthless. No-one would or could claim that he was anything other than honest, however. The 'sharp' referred solely to his cut-throat approach to business, not that he indulged in any kind of shady operations.

It should, therefore, come as little, if no, surprise that he enjoyed this reputation and took great pride in always being seen to live up to this picture. Revelling in it would be too strong, too self-indulgent; he was no basking shark, after all. He was a Shortfin Mako Shark, swift, nimble and always alert to an opportunity.

And so it was that Sidney was cruising the waters of his bay, for there were very few who would dare to venture an opinion which sought to contradict that it was actually 'his' bay. The athleticism in his every movement was grace personified; indeed, it was hard to reconcile the knowledge that such poise and beauty could harbour such focused intent and steely determination. It was whilst he was slicing through waves, deciding to visit the surface that he caught a glimpse of Walter the Whale, some way off in the distance.

Now, Sidney was afraid of no one; there was no one he would not face, but he would rather not have bumped into Walter that morning. There was a small financial business between them that Sidney had not yet resolved. And so, with a streamlined curve and a desire to move downward to the lower depths, he assumed the arc of a diver, and a very graceful one at that, as he swam swiftly into darker and murkier waters. In truth, he was a little put out as he had been enjoying his cruise on the surface. It was a beautiful day and there was little he enjoyed more, business deals aside, than the warming sun on his smooth, slippery back as he surveyed both skyline and the water below. Still, it was not to be today. As he was reflecting on the change of direction, both literally and metaphorically, that his day had taken, Sidney noticed a lone, forlorn figure perched atop a large rock encrusted with shells.

Whilst deep to you and I, the waters as this point were still relatively shallow. Sidney's laser-like eyesight identified the troubled figure as being one Ollie the Octopus. As this was an unscheduled meeting, and an unexpected item in his hastily rearranged morning agenda, he decided to investigate further.

No sooner had he made such a decision than he detected a low, moaning sound which was clearly emanating from the mournful figure in front of him.

"Ollie, my friend, what on earth can be the matter? You don't appear to be yourself at all," he offered, realising at once that something was amiss.

"Oooh, ooooh, ooooooh," wailed the troubled octopus. "Oooh," he continued.

"Please stop this sound, Ollie. Whatever is the matter?" cried a rather concerned Sidney.

"Oooh, Sidney," replied the stricken Ollie. "I have a terrible headache. I can't bear to open my eyes." And with that he reached up with six of his arms and joining with the two which were already clasped on top of his head, ensured that all eight now enwrapped his head as if to protect him from any outward force. His voice subsided to a whimper.

Sidney couldn't leave Ollie in such distress. He quickly thought what could be done and, recalling the beautiful clear air and warming sun, resolved that this was what poor Ollie needed to restore him to full health.

"Ollie," he cried, and quickly resumed in a whisper as the gasp and wince which his exultation brought forth from Ollie made plain just how badly he was suffering. "You need fresh air to clear your airways. You look terribly green about the gills, my old chap." Now, octopus' gills are located just outside the mantle cavity and are not at all easy to see at the best of times, never mind when the said octopus has all its arms raised upward and clasped close to its body and around its head.

Ollie, on hearing Sidney's words, contemplated what he had said and decided that the shark was merely using a figure of speech, but also resolved to check his mantle cavity, once his headache had passed, just to be on the safe side. Green gills were not something

64

with which he wished to be reconciled.

"What's it to be then?" Sidney continued in a more soothing and comforting tone, his bedside manner improving noticeably in just a matter of brief moments. "You jump on my back, hold on with two arms and I'll glide to the surface. You'll be right as rain in no time at all," he promised.

Once again, Ollie was perplexed. His splitting headache did not deter him from considering just what exactly it was about 'rain' which was 'right'. And, if there was anything at all, could its 'rightness' be able to cure creatures who spent their days underwater and would rarely, if ever, feel the rain? Indeed, he considered, would I even know that it was raining? Unsurprisingly enough, such ponderings merely increased the throbbing inside his head.

"Ooooh, ooooh," he wailed, a sound so melancholic and upsetting that he scared himself.

"That's it! I'm taking charge. Get on my back now!" ordered Sidney.

Without further thought which, considering where thought had led him a few moments previously was probably for the better, Ollie peeked out from under one of his arms, pointed a second and third downwards and 'tiptoed' ever so gingerly onto Sidney's back. The shark had manoeuvred himself into a position so close to his stricken friend that the operation was conducted in a matter of seconds.

Ollie clasped hold and they were away. Sidney was careful not to swim too quickly, and his streamlined stroke caused little turbulence for the headache-suffering octopus.

Now Sidney had been thinking carefully and he sensed a great opportunity to be had whilst helping Ollie. He swam with focus and determination, heading out towards the deeper waters, yet rising towards the surface as he did so.

Ollie began to wonder where he was being taken and such wondering seemed to lift his headache. He determined to ask Sidney once they arrived at the surface, deciding the lessening of the throbbing inside his head was, after all, to be greatly welcomed.

The sun glinted from above and around it was an azure blue as Sidney and Ollie split the waters and came to the surface… right in front of Walter the Whale.

Without pausing for breath, Sidney cried out. "Hey, Wally. Here's the sick squid I owe you!"

FOWL PLAY IN THE LIBRARY

Preface

Of course, dear reader, it is God-given that all these tales, and many more like them, have descended by word of mouth. And they have evolved as stories which should be recited aloud; performed, even. As such, each rendition will be different and can have additions or elements modified and removed as befits the occasion or mood.

Any performance will benefit from a depth to the characters involved, and this may well involve different voices or sound effects.... Witness the tale of the Bloody Red Knight on the Bloody Red Horse. A few, however, do require noises and impressions to create exactly the right atmosphere and feeling. For Fowl Play In The Library, a passable (or humorously poor!) impersonation of an excited chicken really does bring the tale to life. The fact that such squawking and general mayhem occurs within a library makes the whole scene just that little bit more ludicrous and surreal. I leave the impressions, noises and general chaotic behaviour to your own imagination and, should you chance to relay the tale, your own ability to convey the sounds and behaviour of a very excited chicken.

The library sat just back from the main road which ran through a not untypical set of suburban dwellings. This community eventually gave way to a far larger town not more than one mile in a northerly direction, separated by a not inconsiderably sized river. This river would become larger before eventually being welcomed by the sea, some 17 miles away. But this aspect of geography and the wider landscape of the area is not the focus of our tale here today. But the landscape, itself, does play its part, for lying directly behind the library, accessed via a number of ladder roads adjoining the main road, lies a more rural setting.

The few suburban roads that led to the fields beyond were home to houses which were set well back from where only a few cars would travel, seeing as each was, to all intents and purposes, a cul-de-sac. The homes were large and clearly wished to hold themselves some distance from the road in order to avoid unwelcome attention. They were happy, secure and contented, and wished that their good fortune and wellbeing was theirs and not something to be displayed to others. In that, it was quite ironic as each was as opulently comfortable as the other and, aside from those who may choose to walk to the fields, the roads were only ever travelled by those whose homes these houses were, or those who chose to visit them.

Sorry, I digress, and that is not my aim. Although, perhaps, it has not been a total digression as our protagonist, the chicken, whom

I shall name Mildred, did pass by these very houses on a number of occasions. Such journeys are very central to the tale... but these journeys are a little way in the distance. Let us go back to the beginning and, to be true, where most of the story plays out. The Library.

As you would expect for such a small, provincial, suburban gathering, the Library was a relatively small, relatively inconspicuous building. Certainly, large enough to satisfy the curiosity and literary desires of those whom it served. In times of cuts in the community, the local council, to their immense credit, acknowledged the importance of such a building. Yes, it had changed and evolved. A small number of computers with six accompanying chairs tucked under a large table upon which they sat, now occupied an annexe room. This had previously been titled the 'Reading Room'; people still read in there, be it the books, the paper, the periodicals or, more likely, the screens of the computers. Very importantly, the 'Children's Corner' had been preserved. When talk of changes had first been mooted, a surprisingly large number of the community had made very clear that removal of this area would be the one thing they would never countenance. I have deliberately used the word 'community', as its members were truly that. A very close community. Many had lived all their lives here; many had also returned after having part or all of their working lives elsewhere. As such, a large number fostered clear and fond memories of the role the 'Children's Corner' had held in their own early childhoods and how they had spent many years when rearing their own children, ensconced in its welcoming and enchanting world. It was theirs and it was for future generations. Yes, the Children's Corner was there and long would it remain. I should add, at this point in proceedings, that it is still there and is still home to the early, wide-eyed discoveries of the many young infants (and, on some occasions, not so young) who treat it as a much-loved home, with great care, affection and respect.

The remainder housed an impressive range of books. Various bookcases stretched their arms towards the reception desk whilst three walls housed the written word from floor almost to ceiling. Seemingly every possible space had been utilised productively. It was hard to imagine how another book, however slim it may be, could find a home here.

Having mentioned the reception desk, it would be remiss of me, at this point, not to mention the two people who were custodians of this treasured land. They were of similar age, early 50s, and both had lived in the community all their lives. Mrs Wilson, or Joan as her identification badge announced, was ever so slightly the sterner of the two.

But in reality, this was more a façade; she loved to welcome people and sought to help in any way she could. Amy, her co-custodian, was, judging by the eye, slightly the younger of the two. But there was no hierarchy here; both were very happy in each other's company. They held a close working relationship and, whilst not as close outside of the library, it could easily be seen that their friendship was as strong as any. Perhaps it was a three-way friendship? Was the library, itself, a silent (Children's Corner aside) partner? It would never have been termed a 'sleeping partner'. And, of course, it then became an extended friendship with all who came to share in what the library, Joan and Amy offered.

I think you now have a very clear picture and understanding of the library and those who share it. And so it was, one fine early summer morning that the beautiful, old, revolving doors gently turned to allow its most recent visitor to enter the hallowed building. But this time it was different. Joan and Amy love little more than welcoming a new face but, true to say, both were somewhat taken aback that, on this occasion, the face belonged to a chicken. To Mildred (not, of course, that they were aware of her name. Indeed, it never became apparent to them that the feathered newcomer had a name. Why would it?) It was enough that a chicken had entered. And this chicken seemed determined; this was no flight of fancy. Assuming, that it is, Mildred could take flight. Which she couldn't.

Mildred proceeded to take steps forward to the reception desk, moving in the way which is so particular to her kind. Her head bobbed forwards and then jerked backwards with each step she took. Joan and Amy remained speechless each casting a sideways glance at each other which asked of them 'What on earth is happening?'

Seemingly unperturbed by the guardians of the building and all its precious books, Mildred strutted past our two custodians and proceeded to head down the aisle which led to 'General Fiction'. At this point, both of the two other visitors to the library suddenly became aware of their newly-arrived companion. One standing, one seated, both, inadvertently let their lower jaw fall and, in what can only be described as a comic action of imitation, slowly lifted their left arms to point at Mildred in silent incredulity. The chicken was not in the least perturbed and continued her progress until faced by a wall of books, the particular section being 20th Century literature, authors DAL-HER. It was here that Mildred halted and with rapid twitching of her head, she clearly began to scan the bookshelves. Whilst concentrating, she began to make that sound which is associated with all chickens, a clucking. In a library it should have registered as an unwelcome disturbance. However, it was early in the day and the few people within the building were still in states of bewilderment. Indeed, it should also be said that Mildred had moderated her clucking to a noise which seemed to suggest a contentment. It was the sort of chicken noise which you may associate with a happy hen as it sits on its brood in a sun dappled henhouse. Knowing that it had laid not one but two eggs and would soon be rewarded with a satisfying breakfast. A mellow, almost indulgent calm had befallen the library when, all of a sudden, Mildred's contented clucking gave way to a flurry of movement and excited squawking. Before either Joan or Amy could move, Mildred had a book tucked under her wing and was making her way to the desk. She stopped at the section of the desk normally reserved for children for it was low set. With a considerable effort, she hopped and flapped and landed on the counter. Mildred carefully placed the book, face up, before her, looked Joan in the eye and, with a nod of her head and 'shadow peck', of her beak, clearly requested the book be stamped so she could be on her way.

What was Joan to do? Mildred clearly wasn't a member. She had no card. There were rules she had to observe but where in all these rules was anything stated about a chicken requesting the loan of a book? She looked to Amy for help, but all she could offer was a slight raise of her eyebrows and shoulders. This was, most definitely, a special case. And so it was that, for the first time ever, she stamped a book and allowed it to begin its outward journey without knowing who was taking it and what their destination.

Mildred reached down and with some difficulty, slipped Ernest Hemingway's 'A Farewell to Arms' under her wing. How apt, thought Joan. Even stranger, thought Amy and both, of course, were correct in their thinking. Mildred crossed the floor clucking: here was a very happy and proud hen. She negotiated the revolving doors with consummate ease, hopped down the three steps which were immediately beyond the doorway, strutted down the short pathway, turned an abrupt right and disappeared from sight.

Without a word, Joan made coffee. All four inhabitants sat drinking before the gentleman visitor, an elderly man in his 80s, questioned whether they had all actually witnessed what each of them knew, very clearly, they had. The elderly lady, possibly as much as 10 years his junior, ventured her opinion that they had, indeed, just seen a chicken take out a library book. It isn't recorded what the names of either of these visitors were, although it is known that they hadn't come to the library together. They were just there, on that day, on that morning, when the incredible and the surreal occurred.

After they finished their coffee and quiet conversation, all fell silent. Each determined that they would not tell another soul what they had witnessed. Who, of course, would have believed them? The quietness remained for the rest of the day, as befits a library. People came and went. Amy left shortly before Joan, as she had a dental appointment at 3.15pm. By the half hour, Joan had set the alarm and locked the large oak door which lay in front of its more excitable revolving cousin. The staid, solemn form of its thick oak body acting as sentinel for all that lay beyond and within. Joan went home.

It would be fair to say that neither of the custodians slept soundly that night. They weren't afraid, nor were they worried... I suppose it may be put down to adrenalin. Yes, adrenalin coursing through their bodies being followed by imaginary chickens whose cries of delight were so bad that it was no wonder that sleep eluded them.

Both Joan and Amy arrived at the library much earlier than was the norm the following day. Indeed, they lived within a minute of each other; Joan still unlocking when Amy scurried up the pathway. So rapt in the previous day's happenings were they that they shared a compartment of the revolving door, something that had never happened before. This meant each had to shuffle their feet to move in time with the slow, circular siding of their vehicle which would, very soon, allow them to alight and be met by the warm welcome of the library. Never 'their' library; no, it belonged to the community.

But if there were persons who could be said to have a closer and more intimate relationship with the sanctuary it would hardly be surprising to learn that it was Joan and Amy.

A fresh cup of coffee was soon warming both their hands. Neither knew what to say: they were both acutely aware of how ridiculous and unbelievable was the episode in which they shared the previous day. But both knew, with absolute certainty, that it did occur. Eventually, after what seemed to be a lengthy, awkward silence, punctuated only by what seemed like little sighs and tuts, interspersed with quiet giggling, they spoke. Neither would actually have been proud to have reflected on the latter; as said, they were not stern-faced librarians who instilled a frosty silence throughout each day. They were gentle, kind and always gave a smile and a polite inquiry as to the welfare of each visitor. They both loved to hear the happy chatter of the early readers in the Children's Corner. But they would always draw the line at indulging inside chatter and quiet laughter between themselves.

"Do you think," Joan whispered, fractionally ahead of Amy whose own offering to their first conversation was, seemingly, an echo of the words of her fellow librarian. Both ceased, looked at each other, and proceeded to giggle once more. Pulling herself together first, Joan continued "Do you think he'll be back? Today?"

Amy quickly pointed out that 'he' was, in all likelihood, 'she', much, no doubt to the approval of the absent Mildred.

"Oh, I do hope so. Wasn't it incredible? A chicken who likes books," her words tumbled out as her eyes widened in amazement. Nodding in agreement, Joan rose and walked to the revolving door. It was time for the library to open to the wider community. It was time for their day to begin.

As she exited the revolving door, approached the outer door and reached for the large key, she became aware of some form of commotion on the other side. In slight trepidation she opened the door, carefully and saw.... Nothing. Nothing that is, until she lowered her gaze to ground level where the sight of a disconsolate chicken, struggling to hold Hemingway's classic novel, startled her.

Mildred looked up, a pained expression replacing the euphoric one which had adorned her face less than a day earlier. Her clucking now had a mournful tone; clearly, all was not well with Mildred. Without thinking, Joan reached down and took the hardbacked copy from beneath the struggling chicken's wing. Mildred seemed to nod a sorry 'thanks' before proceeding into the library followed, dutifully, by Joan. Mildred passed the reception desk, not looking up at the open-mouthed Amy and stalked past with a growing steely determination replacing her woebegone look of moments before. Amy was, secretly, disappointed that Mildred had appeared to ignore her, but she was soon to reflect and realise that Mildred was totally focused on finding a book. Not any book, but 'the' book. This was a bird on a mission.

Joan returned to Amy's side. They looked at each other, askance. Joan merely raising her right eyebrow which was met, in response, with a very slight raising of the shoulders by Amy. Without a word they seemed to determine to bury themselves in whatever administrative work they could find but allowing themselves to listen to the rather doleful clucks of Mildred as she strained her neck, slowly moving up and down the aisles.

Minutes turned into quarter hours which, in turn, beget the half hour marks. A few other visitors arrived, stayed and went. Most incredulous upon seeing a chicken searching for a book, a few oblivious to her presence. The Children's Corner was due to open in just over 15 minutes and an unspoken feeling of worry passed between Joan and Amy. The children were always very well behaved; excitable, yes, but that was only natural. And good. However, what would they be like if they were aware that there was a chicken in the library? Both librarians shuddered at the thought yet as they did, they were startled by a loud squawking which arose from the aisle situated directly to the rear of their desk, behind the only PC which sat in their area. This lone PC was a topic of frustration for both Joan and Amy who, with more than some justification, believed they merited a computer each. It would certainly help them to work in a more speedy and efficient fashion. However, with so many cuts in the funding to such establishments, they had agreed not to raise the issue for fear that any revelation may lead to sole occupancy for one of them whilst the other was asked to leave. Such a thought reduced the sharing of a computer to a mere triviality; indeed, it turned it into something which brought them even closer together.

This time Amy was closer. She hurried to the source of the excitement to be met by an exultant Mildred who was flapping her wings and pointing at a book whilst hovering two to three feet above the floor. She was excited. So was Amy, who moved closer and being careful not to get caught by any part of the chicken's body, tentatively retrieved the desired copy. She looked at Mildred whose excited beaming face reassured her that it was AA Milne's 'Toad of Toad Hall' which was the book that Mildred wanted. Taking it straight to the desk, Mildred squawked and flapped her pleasure. Amy stamped the book but, once again, its departure was not actually recorded on the system. Handing it down to Mildred, the grateful chicken nodded her thanks and, clucking with pride, exited the library, navigating the revolving doors as if a seasoned customer. Her proud strut revealed to any observer, of which there were very few, her contentment. She slipped out of sight, having turned right at the end of the path and would soon be at the next right turn, all before the first of the children and parents arrived. For that, both Joan and Amy were greatly relieved. They had to turn their attention to the Children's Corner and for the next two hours they had little time to think of anything else.

After lunch, a relative calm (in fact, a very obvious calm) had descended. Joan looked at Amy, and with a clear sense of determination in her voice she announced.

"Amy, we've got to know what's happening. Aren't you amazed and curious?"

Amy nodded, waiting for Joan to continue, which she duly did.

"If that chicken comes back tomorrow and takes out another book, I'm going to follow him... her," she corrected herself on seeing Amy's expression. "We'll know where she's going and what she's doing."

Amy nodded again, this time showing her approval.

It was a plan. They sat back, happy in the knowledge that they would, she hoped, soon be able to fathom this mysterious visitation. The books? Well, the copy of a Farewell To Arms had been returned in good condition; neither librarian would claim that the works under their care were in any kind of danger. But what was happening to them? What was the chicken doing with these books? And why these books in particular? The thought of knowing the answers to these questions made both Joan and Amy relax.

The rest of the afternoon seemed to slip by and they soon found themselves outside the library, the main door locked behind them. And with a quick nod of reassurance, accompanied by a ghost of excitement in their eyes, they went their separate ways. Both Joan and Amy only had thoughts for the following day and the hoped-for return of Mildred.

If the day before had been one of excited speculation, on the next morning the rising sun brought with it a mood of wishful thinking and fevered anticipation. She'd be back, wouldn't she? Would she be happy? But if she was happy, wouldn't that mean she was satisfied with Toad and Mole and company and, surely, that would mean she'd still be reading the book? Not even a chicken can read that quickly?!

Looking back, Amy couldn't in all honesty say which of the above questions brought her back down-to-earth with more than a little bump. She feared that it was, in truth, not until contemplating the various speed at which a chicken could read, that the more-than-surreal nature of her thoughts dawned upon her. Whatever it was, she was consumed with a dread that Mildred would not travel through the revolving doors in the day that lay ahead of her. Perhaps she would never return? Amy felt herself bite her lip as a small, but detectable shiver ran down her spine, replacing the longed-for feeling of anticipation with an aching longing, bordering on desperation.

Joan felt the same as both confided their hopes and fears as they arrived outside the library a clear 30 minutes before it was due to open for business. The key that sat in Joan's hand felt heavy and cumbersome; it took her three separate attempts to get it to click into place and allow her to push open the heavy door. The particular musty smell of all libraries seemed mustier than normal. Whatever it was, the 'it' didn't seem quite right. The time was out of joint. Both Joan and Amy felt it and both, without voicing their feelings, wished that these feelings were not some portent for the day ahead.

Their nervousness was such that they concluded, independently of each other, that they would be better to focus on their own small tasks until they opened the library. And this they succeeded in doing, although neither could remember a time before, of after, come to that, when they opened the big, imposing outer door to welcome their customers before the allotted hour. But this Joan did, a full five minutes before the scheduled opening time. If she thought she would be greeted by a chicken, full of sorrow or joy, she was sadly mistaken. The pathway which led from the library was empty.

Joan turned slowly and, she would have to admit, with a sense of despondency and dejection. She reappeared as the revolving door seemed to push her out, such was her reluctance to re-enter without being accompanied by a chicken. Amy could see that her friend was crestfallen and shared the feeling. Where was Mildred?

Time crawled up the hour and seemed to dig its heels in as it traced an equally dilatory descent. Each customer who entered was not greeted by the usual warm smile but in its place lay a rather wan, pale reflection of the normal beam. It was still kind and not enough for anyone to take offence or draw any conclusions, but it wasn't the same.

Three or four of the library's regulars shared the feeling. They had witnessed Mildred's visits and were also harbouring their own wishes to witness her return. The morning reached its apex and appeared to hover before deciding that it would, after all, embrace the afternoon. The small amount of lunch that Joan and Amy tried to eat seemed tasteless and hard to swallow. They both soon abandoned the exercise and found some consolation in a cup of tea.

It was as the first taste of tea wet their lips that Amy caught sight of a small figure struggling to escape the clutches of the revolving door. Slowly, deliberately, and with a knowing look cast to Joan, she rose and raced to the door. Pushing ever so gently, she allowed the prisoner to be freed, but never did a released inmate look so mournful. A plaintive cry, neither a cluck nor a squawk, came from Mildred's beak. In truth, it seemed to have its source from deep within her body. With disconsolate steps, the chicken made slow progress to Joan at the reception desk. Each step was accompanied by a rhythmical shake of her head. Such was her misery that Joan slipped out from behind the desk and gathered the once desired but now despised book from Mildred's clutches.

The weight having left her, she moved slightly quicker, but her mood was still low and she seemed set for a long spell in the library. It had taken her almost three hours the day before; how long would this afternoon's quest last? Would it result in a successful discovery or would Mildred be destined to leave with no book?

The tension behind the desk and within those customers present was palpable. Every now and then a clucking noise, but it was soon replaced by the more morose mumblings that seemed to fill the whole of the building. Both Joan and Amy were upset; they felt helpless. On a couple of occasions each stole to the end of an aisle and, as unobtrusively as was possible, peered to see what was happening. They need not have been so covert in their operations as Mildred was clearly engrossed in her search for the text she so desperately desired.

And then, when all hope seemed to have been lost, the mood within the building changed abruptly and the air was filled with a squawking of utter joy and delirium. No-one within the vicinity could be in any doubt that happiness reigned. Joan and Amy forgot themselves and clapped their delight before hugging each other. The few customers who had remained, as the misery that had preceded such wild abandonment had caused many to leave, beamed at one another. As Mildred approached the desk with a copy of 'The Observer's Guide To Pond Life' secured firmly under her right wing, beaming and squawking as she strutted along, a cheer broke out which was accompanied by a general round of applause.

Mildred beamed and, in a way only chickens can do, looked somewhat abashed. The valued book was gently taken from beneath her wing by an ever-so-careful and equally ever-so-happy Joan. Once stamped and returned ever-so-carefully to Mildred, the chicken nodded her thanks, turned on her heel, or at least the base of her left claw, and exited the library, clucking contentedly.

No sooner had Mildred vacated the building than Joan was at the hat and coat stand, wrestling with her enthusiasm and trying to extricate her light summer overcoat. "More speed, less haste" giggled her friend, which resulted in a look of mock exasperation as Joan finally completed her Harry Houdini act in reverse by proudly standing and wearing her light blue outer protection.

"I'm going to follow her," she whispered, "and I'll then be able to tell you what this great mystery is all about." Joan simply could not hide her excitement, but as she turned to leave she remembered to add. "You will be alright here, on your own, won't you?"

Amy smiled her reply, "Of course. Now get going. I simply must know what lies at the bottom of our chicken's visits." It did not escape the attention of Amy, or even Joan as she entered the revolving door, that Amy's use of the collective personal pronoun revealed just how much Joan's task meant to them both. Mildred was, in a special way, their chicken. She had chosen their library; she had come and gone; sought their assistance. Yes, Mildred, deserved to be thought of as 'our' mused Amy.

Joan cut a most unlikely spy as she scurried down the pathway which led to the entrance from the main road. She caught her enthusiasm and, halting just in time, she stopped behind the large, right hand gate pillar. Craning her neck forwards, she peeped amid its furthest edge and looked along the pavement.

Joan was just in time to see Mildred execute a sharp and jaunty right turn to move into the first side road. She had to contain herself and with a greater self-discipline than she had enacted for many a year, Joan counted slowly to 20 before stepping gingerly out onto the pavement and following in Mildred's recent tracks, not that they were physically visible. In truth, from 13 onwards, she had found herself counting just a little bit quicker. Joan contained her giggles as she found herself thinking that the last time she had done something similar was when playing 'hide and seek' as a pupil at the local primary school. She also found that she was experiencing the same frisson of excitement and expectation. Anyone watching her would have been incredulous at the sight of the smartly-dressed lady scurrying along on tiptoe in shoes with a two-inch heel. Occasionally, she would slow before taking two or three theatrical steps, placing her weight on her toes as she stalked

Mildred with great stealth.

On reaching the side road, Joan executed the same move she had enacted when she was at the main gate, no more than two minutes earlier. Mildred was already a good 70 yards down the pavement Joan estimated, before correcting herself to 75 to 80 metres. She wanted to embrace all modern measurements but, in truth, always thought in yards or gallons or miles per hour before having to conduct a mental feat of conversion. As mentioned, in the introduction to this tale, the houses here were large, with quite imposing driveways. Some had gates which were firmly shut to outsiders. This was one of the most affluent areas in a relatively comfortable small suburb. This meant that Joan had to be very careful; her options for darting behind a hedge or gatepost were few and far between. Fortunately, the road dipped and soon Mildred disappeared from sight. Of course, the relief was temporary as Joan immediately worried that she would lose Mildred. By hurrying to the brow, she could see that Mildred had continued her forward march but Joan was now exposed. At this very moment, Mildred stopped. She carefully lowered her precious cargo to the ground before stretching upwards and craning her neck to the sky and stretching out her wings. Whilst doing so, she turned round to look at where she had recently travelled… As luck would have it, Joan saw what was happening and was able to hop into one of the few driveways which remained open to the pavement. She breathed heavily and waited, not daring to steal a glance at Mildred until she was certain that the determined chicken would have continued her journey.

Time seemed to have stopped, everything went into slow motion, even the way in which Joan peered through the privet leaves of the large hedge which adorned the border of the dwelling's estate.

Mildred had, indeed, continued on her way, this time with the book under her other wing. She had made quite impressive progress and was nearing the end of the cul-de-sac. Mildred's sense of intrigue grew yet stronger. Stepping out from behind her hiding place, she moved swiftly in pursuit of Mildred, noticing that she chicken had moved across the road. ('Why did the chicken cross the road?' Joan couldn't help asking herself, stifling a laugh). Meanwhile, Mildred was about to enter a public footpath which ran adjacent to the final, rather imposing homestead.

Mildred was soon out of her sight and, with a growing feeling of concern at losing the destination of her quarry, Joan hurried on moving more into the open, no longer fearing her detection. The public footpath provided ample opportunities to make ground on Mildred, it being enclosed on either side by bushes, trees and a form of hedge. Joan slowed her pace as she realised all of a sudden, that she was only 20 metres from Mildred. The chicken had come to a stile which, once navigated, led into a rather overgrown field which had a pathway beaten down leading to another stile situated in a small hedge at the far side. Mildred hopped up, over and down, very carefully pushing the book through the gap in the stile. Joan witnessed and marvelled, reasoning that Mildred had executed this manoeuvre before, so sure was she in her movements.

Once Mildred was almost halfway across the field, Joan moved to the stile and carefully negotiated its steps. Once in the field there was no natural cover; yes, the grass was high but not that high. She didn't want to dirty her clothes and also considered how she had not envisaged that her journey could take her into such terrain. Still, she couldn't stop now; not when she had come this far. And still with no answer to her burning question. With a comical stealth she lifted each leg far higher than was the case for her normal gait, and with pantomime tread she followed Mildred's path.

By this time, the chicken had now cleared the second gate and was entering a smaller field. This enclosure had some bushes and near its centre was a large pond. In fact, the pond was the main part of the enclosure with the land which surrounded it forming, perhaps, a third of the overall area. For most of the year, the field would be a damp, wet bog of a place but this spring had been very warm and the early days of summer had become hotter still. The ground was rutted as the previously squelched mud had hardened and, eventually, dried out to form an uneven surface which meant that walking upon it was somewhat hazardous. That is, of course, for the human footfall not so that of the chicken. Mildred strutted through, her clucking now giving way to excited squawks.

Joan was over the second stile before she knew it; she could sense that her quest was near its conclusion and she certainly did not want to miss out on its denouement. Her choice of footwear made the very final part of her journey far more difficult than it might have been. Nevertheless, she was a mere 15 metres behind Mildred when the chicken stopped at the edge of the pond and let out a loud and throaty cry. It was obvious to Joan that Mildred was trying to attract someone's attention. Nothing stirred. Once again, Mildred let out her squawked cry, following it up with a continued excited garble which revealed her happiness. Sometime during this garbling, she took the copy of 'The Observer's Guide to Pond Life' from beneath her wing and, much to Joan's dismay and chagrin, seemed to throw it upon the dry ground in front of her. This complete, Mildred let out one final carousing cry and took a step backwards.

Suddenly Joan was aware that from the far side of the pond there was a splash. The sound was echoed, each time getting louder as, whatever or whoever it was, traversed the water using the abundance of vegetation within the pond as occasional landing pads. All at once, and with a most impressive hop, a large frog (or perhaps it was a small toad, as this classification was not in Joan's experience) landed in front of Mildred with only the copy of 'The Observer's Guide to Pond Life' face up, lying between them.

Mildred squawked, chorusing her cries in, what now sounded, more of a hopeful rather than exultant tone.

The large frog, for that is what Joan decided it was, looked at Mildred, looked down at the book and then, returned her focus upon the waiting chicken. The frog's expression of curiosity had turned to one of resignation as he cleared his throat and announced "Reddit!"

THE AUDITION:
PAWS FOR THOUGHT

So where do we stand on celebrity shows? Or, perhaps, just celebrities? What is it to be a celebrity? How much talent does one have to have? Or how little? What, just what, is the attraction? And, leading on from these rhetorical searchings, why is there a craving for such status? Why the desire for this vacuous life with its emptiness and lack of purpose? Heaven protect us from the C and D list celebrities, walking oxymorons, privately glad to have gained their oxy-ness.

But talent shows. Now there you have a difference. Clearly, the word 'talent' is somewhat of a giveaway in this. And, true, there are many shows in which people with no shame, and even less of the aforementioned talent, lay themselves open to ridicule. Is the incredulity their performance attracts, itself, enough? And are we to blame? Can we smugly mock or claim to be horrified and embarrassed if we actually watch such offerings? Are we no better? In fact, are we worse? But, as I said, there can be a difference. There are many 'acts' which display tremendous talent; they are truly awe-inspiring and worthy of attentive adulation.

And then, there are those acts who could and should have made it but don't. The fickle finger of fate points elsewhere and seems to only wave at the poor unfortunate; fame and riches or its underbelly not being granted to them. Some incredible talent is destined never to reach a wider audience. For some, it will destroy them; for others, it saves them from destruction. And for a few, a very few, they are simply left bemused by it all. Let me introduce you to Rufus.

I've always felt Rufus was a great name. It conjured up an image of someone who trod their own path in life, an outsider, a bit of a rebel, someone who cared not one jot for what others felt and so had an aura of 'cool' about them. And so it was for this Rufus. That he was a dog mattered not at all. That he was a shaggy, long-haired mutt of indeterminate breed, also did not matter. He was Rufus. And Rufus had talent. He also had Nigel, who laboured under the misapprehension that he owned Rufus. The very thought made Rufus chuckle in his canine-like way, but he tolerated Nigel as the man was kind-hearted and provided a home and food. Yes, Nigel also knew that Rufus had talent.

The story itself is, mercifully, pretty short. There are no twists, turns or dead-ends and no soul-searching, anger, misery or tears of a tortured soul. Just bewilderment.

Rufus and Nigel had been into town, something which did not happen very often as neither much liked the commercial or industrial areas. But on this occasion, Nigel had needed to visit his solicitor as he was finalising the legal requirements to becoming a Power Of Attorney for his Aunt Claire who, sadly, was living in a care home and beginning to show signs of being confused and forgetful. Rufus thought she must, indeed, be very confused and forgetful to entrust her estate and well-being to Nigel and, far from the first time in his life and their acquaintance, he pondered on the stupidity of a society which entrusted important decisions to simpletons such as Nigel whilst overlooking the more astute and far-sighted dogs of this world of which he was one.

I should also take a bit of an issue with the claim that Nigel had visited 'his' solicitor. It was a solicitor who was recommended when he was suddenly confronted with his new and daunting responsibility. That was their second visit and, in all likelihood, there would not need to be another until nature took its course with Aunt Claire. So, 'his solicitor' is stretching it more than a little. But if Nigel chose to think this way and if it made him walk that little bit taller, then what harm could there be in that? Certainly, that was how Rufus viewed it.

Now, as this was only their second visit, and to a part of town that was not familiar to either Rufus or Nigel, they trekked through the streets taking in new sights. The solicitors' practice was in a rather affluent and well-to-do block which, curiously enough, gave way to a notably seedier area which seemed to harbour more than its fair share of gambling premises and public houses whose clientele had poured onto the pavement, even by midmorning. One such establishment had wrought iron tables and chairs with an accompanying warning that they were under the eye of CCTV in a somewhat misguided and deluded attempt to create a bohemian atmosphere.

However, this whimsical attempt had, by chance, lent a more natural setting for its bedfellow. 'Carwell's Talent Agency' proclaimed its relationships with stars of stage, screen and, well, celebrities. Nigel stopped abruptly and took great deliberation reading the names on Mr Ryman Carwell's books. He whistled quietly to himself. And then he stopped. He looked down at Rufus, purely because he stood taller as in every other way, the boot would firmly have been on the other foot. Rufus edged away and resolutely shook his head. Nigel stepped towards him and said, in his most coaxing and soothing voice, "Come on, boy. You know you want to really. You're brilliant; together we will go down a storm!"

Rufus raised a quizzical eyebrow at the word, 'together'. This was, indeed, worse than he had feared; not only was his mutton-brained partner going to make him jump through some ghastly metaphorical hoops, but he intended to be the one holding them. 'Nothing but shame,' he reasoned. To quote Shakespeare was not in itself unusual for Rufus, although even he began to feel some of that shame in comparing his predicament to that of the Dauphin at the hands of the youthful King Henry V. "Think of being on television", continued a clearly star-struck Nigel, "we will be on the chat shows, Hello magazine, perhaps a movie contract will follow...." Nigel drifted into reverie. Rufus tried to drift away, but he had to face the unpalatable truth that his destiny was about to be thrown in front of the querulous Mr Carwell. And despite displaying a marked reluctance to pass through the door, he duly followed Nigel.

The pair, once outside the door which gave way to the street, were faced with a steep staircase. A sharp turn to the left, after 18 steps, led to a further six before the landing was made. In front of them was a huge, dark brown door with a bevelled glass panel, below which was a placard which read 'Ryman Carwell: Starmaker." Nigel nodded slowly; Rufus, once again, raised an eyebrow, this time at the sheer front of Mr Carwell. He had hoped that the boldness of such a claim might have stopped the usually reticent and unassuming Nigel in his tracks; made him consider the enormity (and foolhardiness) of taking a step into the Carwell lair and humbly beat a well-considered retreat back into the real world, its normality, anonymity and safety. But it would seem the lure of fame and fortune had rendered him incapable of clarity of thought. What had he done? Rufus, for once, had been too slow to respond. In the everyday swing of things, he was always two or three steps ahead of Nigel; granted, this wasn't saying much. He shook his head dolefully; trying hard to dismiss the troubling thought that Nigel's own train of thought had been clearer and more purposeful. If misguided and ridiculous. For once, Rufus would have to play the role of the follower, whilst still looking for every opportunity to prevent what would be a terrible humiliation. For them both!

The waiting room which led to Mr Carwell's office was surprisingly understated. No ostentatious trappings of wealth but in its place were the genial smiles of the 'oh so nearly' famous glinting from the frames on the wall as their eyes, in their brightness, cast doubt and disdain that any visitor could contemplate the thought that they would be able to follow in their hallowed footsteps.

Miranda's voice called out the kind of 'hello' which translates, not so politely, as 'and what on earth brings you here?' The slight note of incredulity and distaste being unable to be held from her delivery. Nigel blustered: Miranda cut an imposing figure. Not too difficult when set against the apologetic frame of Nigel but, in truth, she was quite startling; both in her formal presentation and her looks. Rufus decided she was extremely good looking, rather than beautiful. He certainly wasn't the sort to judge anyone on their looks alone or to deny beauty due to someone's years. Miranda, he judged, was to be just the other side of 50. It troubled him greatly that the more he considered his judgement, the more he could only think that she had been truly beautiful and not so long ago. He had some serious thinking to do; he didn't like how he had arrived at his assessment. Perhaps the saving grace had been the slightly icy tone to her 'hello'. Yes, that must be it. Relieved that he wasn't someone who judged beauty by youth,

Rufus relaxed.

His state of relaxation vanished as soon as it had made its presence known. Nigel was still blustering and in danger of being shown the door before he could fully explain why the pair of them had entered the premises in the first place.

Finally, he strung together the seemingly outrageous statement 'Hello, I'd like, or rather, we'd like to see Mr Carwell, please. Rufus, my dog."

At this, Rufus bristled and let out what could only be described as a contemptuous cough.

"Rufus speaks. He's a talking dog."

Rufus looked at Nigel and very slowly shook his head pitifully. He then turned his gaze upon Miranda, raised one eyebrow, as was clearly his habit, and gave her his 'What can you do?" look.

Miranda was rendered speechless, not so much by the apparent audacity of Nigel's claim. Rufus believed she must have borne witness to many such claims and a great many which were even more fanciful. Of course, he did have the advantage of knowing that he could, indeed, talk. But, nevertheless, he imagined far wilder and more far-fetched utterances being projected to the once excited and gradually more jaded and cynical Miranda. It was Rufus' expression which revealed his total pity for Nigel and a world-weariness that he was expected to be part of a music hall double act.

Double Act, of course, included Nigel. Rufus tolerated this; he was well aware that Nigel possessed less talent than almost anyone he had met. Miranda seemed to sense this. Not the bit about Nigel: of that she had been painfully aware before he had even opened his mouth.

As fate, or terrible coincidence, would have it, a door opened and a rather unnaturally tanned figure, sporting a light white T-shirt, faded jeans and deck shoes, entered the room. "Did anyone really wear deck shoes?" thought Rufus.

"Mr Carwell," stuttered Nigel. Before continuing "I'm Nigel." That much information was, of course, not going to satisfy Mr Carwell. In fact, it didn't satisfy anyone. Even Nigel. It was now Mr Carwell's turn to raise a quizzical eyebrow and, in so doing, he went up, ever so slightly in Rufus' estimation. "It's my dog," Nigel continued.

"Your dog?" Mr Carwell's tone already verged on exasperation which he wasn't really struggling to conceal.

"My dog," Nigel repeated. "Rufus. He talks."

"He talks?" Mr Carwell repeated. Inwardly, Rufus found this to be quite humorous. The well-known celebrated starmarker being struck almost speechless by Nigel. 'Perhaps he did have some talent?' mused Rufus. 'No, silly thought' he just as quickly concluded.

"I thought. **We** thought," Nigel corrected himself, looking at Rufus and wishing for some support. "You might like to know."

Mr Carwell, or Ryman, as Miranda called him when not acting as his PA, shot Miranda a look which clearly questioned how she could have allowed such a fool to enter into conversation, albeit a one-sided conversation, with him. Miranda, to her credit, held his look and returned with a volley of her own which could so easily be interpreted as, "You came in here, of your own free will. Don't blame me. I didn't invite this halfwit in to talk to you."

However, her stare softened as she seemed to indicate that there was something about Rufus.

Mr Carwell turned his attention to Rufus and immediately recognised that there was something about him. He didn't work with animals but if the talent was there, he could always be persuaded to change such a stance. Nigel would have to go, of course. He wouldn't be part of any deal.

In a move that surprised him, he said, "You've got two minutes. Come with me." Nigel was dumbstruck and could scarcely get his limbs to work, but somehow stumbled after the retreating form of Mr Carwell. Rufus blew out his cheeks and whilst padding softly after the other two, he turned his head to Miranda and slowly closed his right eye. Opening it a fraction of a second later, he turned his head to face in the direction in which he was going, gave a wag of his tail and entered Mr Carwell's office.

"He just winked at me," thought Miranda. What was more surprising than this thought was the fact that she wasn't surprised. She stared after Rufus in a way which she had never stared after anyone else who had entered that room. Not even Ryman, himself, she was forced to concede.

Once inside his office, Mr Carwell proceeded straight to business. It was his domain and his rules. He was the starmaker; these hopefuls needed him. Sure of himself, he turned to Nigel and Rufus and offered them seats with a flick of his left hand.

Nigel and Rufus were seated close to one another. Nigel was

nervous and his anxiety was not helped by the rather dismissive. "Well?" which was the only further word to pass Mr Carwell's lips.

Nigel turned slightly to his left before Rufus. He looked, imploringly, at him. Rufus returned his look in the most encouraging manner he could fashion. For all of Nigel's shambolic behaviour he did care for him. He was loyal, friendly and reliable. And so was Rufus.

"Rufus, old friend, please tell me what do we have on the top of our house?"

Rufus feigned thinking, in a most plausible way, before replying with a confident "Roof!"

Encouraged by such rapid and engaging conversation, Nigel quickly continued "Rufus, please tell us what the North Sea is like in winter?"

Without a moment's hesitation, Rufus replied, "Rough!" Nigel looked earnestly at him as if to say that the winter was a fierce one. This elicited a prompt "Rough! Rough!" as a dramatic growl.

It was, perhaps, this rather loud growling of the word which masked the sound of a snapping pencil. Mr Carwell, who wasn't famed for his patience, had clearly seen and heard enough. But Nigel was oblivious to this and was in full flow. "Rufus, what do we have on the outside of trees?" At this point, the tale takes a temporary surreal twist as Rufus' response was to be phonetic to make his point. He barked, offering a simple "Bark!"

"Get out! Get out!" cried Mr Carwell, the vein in his left temple pulsing as it became far more prominent than had been the case before he had made the acquaintance of Nigel and Rufus. Both Rufus and Nigel left their seat but in so doing, Nigel managed a final question for Rufus.

"Rufus, tell Mr Carwell what many French people make from grapes. Indeed, they are famous the world over for doing this." The questions didn't seem to calm Mr Carwell or soothe his temper. Indeed, it could be said to have completely the opposite effect. Once again, allowing the surreal to create the phonetic, Rufus stopped his retreat from the room, sat down and whined. "Whine," this was one of poignancy offering a tale of desolation.

Nigel reached out for the door handle, turned it and fled across the waiting room with Rufus at his heels. Mr Carwell wasn't far behind them. The feeling of fury most evident as he considered himself to have been duped and ridiculed. He, Ryman Carwell, humiliated in his own office. He could scarcely believe it. Miranda was shocked and not a little disappointed to see Rufus disappear through the doorway with the bevelled glass. Nigel and Rufus leapt the six stairs to land only just avoiding a low flying, well-aimed deck shoe which crashed into the wall behind them. Sensing his anger, they headed down the staircase, but in their haste became entangled and landed in a shambolic heap at the bottom.

Seeing them there, Mr Carwell chose to pick up his shoe and vent his anger only in words.

"Never, ever darken my door again!"

With that he turned on what would have been his heel had he been wearing his shoe and slammed the door behind him.

Nigel was crestfallen; his dream lay in tatters around him. Rufus could see his disappointment but could only say," What did I do wrong?"

TO BE FRANK

The following tale should serve as a warning to us all. We live in a land of bureaucracy, spending time filling in forms online and having details checked or checking details ourselves. We curse this. More often than not, we are justified in so doing. But, on occasions, those checks are what protect us and our society from unspeakable horrors. One such tale will now unfold. There are scenes which are unpleasant, their nature and content are deeply disturbing. I have taken care not to be gratuitous in the way I relay these incidents to you and can only hope that I have been successful in my aim. But please be warned, this tale tells of some disagreeable and, seemingly, wicked incidents. I will let you be the judge.

It is the early seventies in San Francisco, not long after the Summer of Love. But what you are about to hear has very little love within it. The heady days of peace, free love and a desire for the common good seem to have given way to desires of a base level and self-interest replacing the dream of a community in which peace and understanding were at the centre.

And yet, whilst I say this, the very anti-hero of our tale clearly possessed qualities which made him likeable, welcoming, helpful and, seemingly, a good friend. He exhibited these on many occasions but… well. I am getting ahead of myself.

It all started in the Western Quarter of San Francisco in the late summer of 1973.

You'll know well the tramcar system of public transport which served the citizens of the community; you'll have probably seen it in many movies or American cop and law enforcement shows. Well, I ask you to picture it and listen carefully to the once forgotten but gradually more familiar sound of the rattling of the tram car as it rides, uniquely characterising the slopes of the city. Hear it wail as its brakes are tried again and again to bring it to a stop. Witness the passengers disembarking and alighting before the whole dance begins once more.

It was here, in the Western Quarter, that Frank worked. Strangely enough, history does not detail his surname and, given what was to occur, perhaps this was a conscious decision and an attempt in which Frank and his actions could be erased from memory and history. It failed!

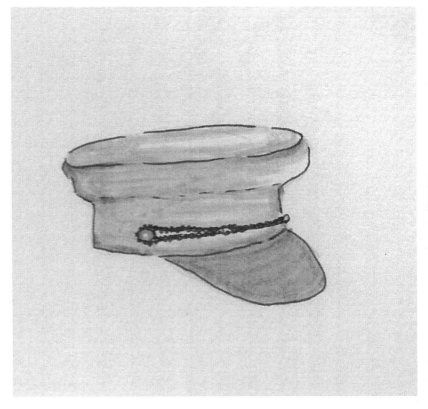

Frank wore the pale blue uniform, as did all employees of the Western Quarter Tram Company. He was always immaculately presented and wore his uniform with pride; he loved his job!

Indeed, his job was his life. And he was so, so good at it. So why, oh why, did it happen? How could he have done it? It is a question which plagued and tormented so many people. It may even have had the same effect on Frank himself. In every other way, on every other occasion, on every other day he was exemplary in his conduct.

As this point I really should make his everyday conduct clear. Before what happened, happened. Frank had worked for the Western Quarter for two months shy of two years. I say worked: I'm not sure Frank would have deemed it such; he saw it as his calling. A true servant of the community, called to help all. And he did just that. And he was loved by all who travelled with him on the number 27. He really was; it is this fact which makes the whole tragedy so… well… tragic.

Frank helped people on and off, guiding the very young and the elderly to their seats. He carried their bags for them. He knew their names, their family members' names. He sang songs and managed to get them to join in with him. Nobody's birthday was ever missed, with the friendly rendition of 'Happy Birthday' sounding loud and clear as the occupants joined with Frank to make that person's day just that little bit more special.

He would talk to newcomers, explaining to them the quickest way to navigate the system in order to get them to their desired destination. He collected the fares, gave them their tickets and both people in the arrangement sailed through the transaction. Yes, Frank was the best. He never had a day off with illness, always punctual even if he was feeling a little under-the-weather. Always full of zest and energy. Put simply, if you'd have ridden his tram you would not have noticed any difference. Frank was exceptional, day in, day out. The Employee Of The Month award became somewhat of a redundant exercise at the Western Quarter. It was always Frank. So it is no surprise he was named Employee Of The Year in his first year and had, seemingly, retained the award for the second year. It was a certainty. But if this tale tells us anything (and it tells us many things), it is that there is no certainty in life. What seems fixed, an ever-present mark, immoveable, can shift in the blink of an eye. The Northern Star which was Frank, a guiding light and a beacon of hope for so many, was about to fall. And when Frank fell, he fell from a great height.

It was a Tuesday. Not that the day itself had any bearing on Frank or his behaviour. He himself, conceded this. That it was a Tuesday when the horrific event occurred is a documented fact. But it could have been any other working day of any other working week. Fate allowed it to fall on this Tuesday. Everyone who offered an opinion on what happened and why, and they were a lot clearer when discussing the former; everyone agreed that the day itself held no influence in proceedings.

Frank had just sat down, the tramcar was approximately two thirds full; it was stated that there were 36 passengers aboard. Frank had been regaling them with a happy song. He was adamant that it was 'Yellow Submarine' and many aboard paid testament to this and yet there were three other songs given in witness testimony, these people swearing that Frank had sung this before sitting down to what was a customary round of applause. Strange how the memory will play tricks or deceive. But the song itself is of little, or no, importance. The mood? Well that, it was thought, was of significance. All were united in saying, that they were all just that; united in a happy, convivial feeling. Frank testified to being a part of that feeling, his modesty and humility not allowing him to consider that he had been the one to create it.

He could also find no reason as to why he would be the one to end it so abruptly.

As the number 27 trundled towards the sixteenth step on the 37-stop circuit, including its destination which was, also, its starting point, an elderly lady stood to make ready to disembark. Frank was on his feet and at her side before she had fully straightened.

"Allow me, Jean," he said, taking her bag and offering his arm as a means by which she could steady herself and be guided to the exit. The pair moved slowly to the rear and Frank used his left hand to hold the pole whilst his right was held firmly by Jean. The tram exit (and entrance, it being one and the same) were open to the air. This was a factor which the courts were to consider and pass judgement upon. However, all trams, in all the four companies and four quarters, were designed to be such. These were also the heady days before 'Health and Safety' edicts were placed firmly at the forefront of any planning design and creation. But, as I intimated at the outset, such freedom comes at a price. Sometimes if can be a heavy price.

On the Tuesday in question it is difficult to put any figure on that price.

Frank carefully unwrapped Jean's arm from his and with his right arm now free, he placed his hand in the small of her back and gave the unsuspecting Jean a small, but purposeful, shove. Jean, being frail, elderly and oblivious to Frank's intentions, simply sailed through the air until her forehead met the sidewalk with a sickening splitting sound, some 10 metres before the tramcar came to rest at stop number 16. The driver, Charlie, was totally unaware of what had occurred at the rear of his tram.

Time stopped. All went still. It wasn't until then that anybody seemed to react to what some had seen. Others, of course, were like Charlie and totally unaware of the demise of Jean. For, at this point, I should make clear that Jean died almost instantly the moment her skull made contact with the concrete. The medical evidence given at court stated that she would have felt little, if anything, and suffered no pain. Small mercies, you may think.

The screams pierced the air, accompanied by the footfall of the man who had been waiting at the tram stop and Frank, himself, who both rushed to the aid of the already deceased Jean. Frank seemed almost to be disbelieving as to what had happened and that he was the cause of it. He wept by the lifeless body of Jean as a dark crimson stream spilt from her open head and wrote her end of life story on the sidewalk.

The police (or 'cops' I should say) were called. Who actually did this no-one seemed to remember. It was well before the appearance of cell phones so not traceable. But a conscious decision must have been taken by somebody or bodies. It may, of course, have been undertaken by another person unfortunate enough to be within the vicinity at the very moment Jean's journey was ended, along with her life.

A dumbfounded and heartbroken Frank was handcuffed, placed in the rear of the police car (I'll refer to them as police, if you don't mind) and taken to the station. Little is actually documented of the time between Jean's death and the trial. Frank did not post for bail; he failed to come to terms with what he had done but did not seek to deny it. The voices of so many of the tram's occupants, his friends, told him of his actions. In court, on hearing each witness testimony, he could only lower his already low head and weep silently.

Frank did not seek to defend himself. He placed a guilty plea and whilst his counsel offered a convincing case for 'grounds of diminished responsibility' which was also strengthened by the very many character witnesses who left no stone unturned in their desire to give the court the most favourable and honest picture of Frank. Perhaps it was the rather confusing circumstance of the character witnesses largely being the self-same people who offered the damning witness testimonies which prevented the judge accepting and supporting the plea. His decision was 'murder in the first degree' – a verdict for which the death sentence was mandatory. The gallery howled in anguish as the judge delivered his judgement with the greatest of solemnity. Frank was taken away, head bowed, without a backward glance.

Despite the pressure coming from his counsel and the fact that he could still recall nothing of the fateful incident, the scene described, time and again in court, held no recollection in his mind. To all intents and purposes, he was truly not there and didn't do what a version of him did do. Despite all this, he refused to lodge any kind of appeal, seeming to wish his fate upon himself, no doubt believing that this was justice and justice must be done, and seen to be done.

Nevertheless, the legal wheels still ground slowly and it was another five months before a shaven-headed Frank was visited, firstly by a Priest and then by the Prison Governor. Apocryphal tales are, by their very nature, true, if delivered often in a slightly coloured fashion. The sober-faced governor looked Frank in the eye; this part of his job did not trouble him as much as you may think. He had usually been faced by inmates for whom he could feel little sympathy. On this occasion however, he felt things differently. Frank seemed a normal, lost, gentle soul. Yes, he was aware that appearances could deceive even the most experienced judge of human character, but Frank had been incarcerated in this building, awaiting his fate, for over five months The Governor had also taken great interest in the trial. He felt sorrow and compassion for Frank.

"You have one last request," he whispered. "What can I do for you?"

Frank looked up and, smiling, softly replied, "I'd like a banana please, sir."

The simplicity of the request added to the emotion the Governor was feeling. He wanted to say more, but words would not come. He nodded, turned on his heels and left to find a banana for the poor man inside the cell. Within a matter of minutes, he had returned and he watched with his face set in a baleful expression as Frank, with care and precision, consumed the banana before declaring himself ready.

Dead man was walking to the chamber where the electric current would be sent through his body. First 25,000 volts and then a second, shorter surge of the same strength. The man tasked with ensuring Frank was seated and strapped into the chair did so in a manner which, as far as could be deemed possible, allowed Frank to retain some dignity. A skull cap was placed on his head and, finally, a hood covered all. All was darkness. Frank remained silent and still throughout. The attendant left the small room.

The lights dimmed. An electronic buzz was heard before the lights flickered back on. The process repeated itself a few moments later. For those in the viewing gallery, no spectators, merely the Governor, attendant and a prison doctor, had they chosen to look, which none of them did, they would have seen Frank's inert body jerk spasmodically as if undertaking a macabre seated dance in time to the music of the current as it coursed through his body.

After what was two or three minutes, all three men entered the room. The hood and skull cap were taken from Frank's head and the doctor held Frank's wrist to test for a pulse, a seemingly futile action and one which would go against all his training. Here he was looking for no pulse; no sign of life. But he was to be surprised for, at the very moment he detected the lightest of pulse beats he was more shaken by a scream of shock and terror from the attendant and the Governor as Frank slowly opened his eyelids to reveal his white rolled-back eyeballs.

Ever so slowly, his eyes, somewhat blood shot, showed themselves. With swollen tongue and parched mouth, Frank uttered the barely audible word, "Water."

"He's alive!" shouted the Governor. Now whether it was these words that were to shape the disgraceful language in the press over the next few years, it is hard to say. But the Doctor's monumental cry from Mary Shelley's gothic horror tale led Frank to be known as 'Frankenstein' or 'Frank, The Monster' or just plain 'Monster' As a side point it was also lazy journalism – Frankenstein was the Doctor, not the monster. An oft-quoted mistake and one the journalists of the sensational and gutter press were so keen to latch upon. But alive he was and another apocryphal tale was seen to be true. If someone were to survive the Death Penalty, they were free to leave; their sentence had been commuted. Frank was a free man.

When I say 'free' he was far from free. His action, which he had resolutely tried to face and had never tried to excuse, continued to haunt him. He still had no real recollection of that horrific day. He hid himself away and that, perhaps, should have been where the story ended. Never ending of course for Frank or those closely affected by the events of that day. But quickly lost by all of us whose own lives and everyday concerns take front seat in our considerations. But the longer time passed, the more Frank sought an answer and the more he missed the interaction with other people and their joys and troubles. He yearned to be back, but he could never go back to…. Well, not to the Western Quarter.

It is a shameful, shameful truth that money and profit is the main motivator in our Western, capitalist society. How else can I seek to explain the fact that, exactly six months to the day that Frank survived the electric chair, he found himself in the dark green uniform of the Eastern Quarter Tram Company. Yes, he had had to fudge a few issues, but it is incredible just how easy it is to sidestep the obstacles which procedures place in your path and also how easy it is to create fictitious references. Of course, a slight irony and absolute truth is that these self-penned testimonials would, in all probability, have been what those who had worked alongside him or been served by him would have written themselves. Aside from one little episode, of course.

But Frank was back. That is an irrefutable fact. And what this sad story records is that, when back, Frank made just the same wonderful impression on route number 9. The passengers quickly grew to love him. His route was jam-packed; frequently people rode the tram solely to listen to Frank. He regaled them with his stories and he listened to them. It was said, at a later court case, that a good few left behind their costly therapy sessions as the ear and advice Frank offered was far, far better. And cost but the price of one of his tickets.

Just as with his days in the Western Quarter, people saw Frank as a friend and a confidante. And just as with his previous employers, his worth caught their eye and he received his full due of thanks and reward. The Eastern Quarter did not run an 'Employee of the Month' scheme. If only they had, this history may well have been prevented from repeating itself. They do now; oh yes, they do now. But I get ahead of myself.

So it was, that on a rather chilly early spring morning almost three years after he had joined the company, Frank was helping two young girls, twins as it happened, to the edge of the tram in readiness for their approaching stop. They knew Frank well and had been explaining what they had just done and how the rest of their day was going to pan out. Frank could recall this most clearly when questioned, but what he had no memory of at all was from the moment his smile had frozen upon his face and he picked both the girls up, one in each hand, cracked their heads together and sent them sailing through the air until their unexpected journey was halted by a sickening collision with the wall of the tram stop shelter. Mercifully, both were dead before they landed on the ground, next to each other as they had been throughout most of their short lives.

Frank returned to a vacated seat and sat, as if in a trance, whilst pandemonium reigned inside and outside the tram. He made no attempt to speak or leave the scene. He was led by the police and walked in a dutiful manner as he was placed in the obligatory squad car before being hurried away.

Of course, as the events of the day were examined, Frank's background was revealed. The gaps in the checks, the slack procedures…. heads did, indeed, roll. Although given what Frank had done that is, I would say, a most inappropriate and insensitive analogy. The press whipped the public into a frenzy. Frank The Monster was a serial killer. He preyed on the very old and the very young; he preyed on the innocent and the vulnerable. He was wicked; he had no conscience; he was, well, he was a monster! And he agreed. He had no defence. He could have no defence. But, just as on that first fateful foray into death and misery, he did have countless character witnesses who paid testament to his selfless, caring and jovial persona. The real Frank could never, ever willingly have done something so evil.

Such testimonies were recognised but couldn't save Frank from a second meeting with the electric chair. And this time there would be no escape, the powers that be announced that Frank was to have 200,000 volts of electricity shot through him for a full 30 seconds. That is a very strong current; enough, as some rather warped thinking observer offered by means of an analogy – 'enough to make a whole field of cows jump up and down'. Quite why he chose such a pastoral setting, and why the cows deserved such treatment is far from clear. But, I suppose, he made some sort of point.

Scrutiny remained on Frank. He made no appeal as, once more, though not recalling anything about the tragic event, he accepted he had committed an horrific crime and deserved his fate. Indeed, he willingly sought to embrace this version as he could no longer be tormented by the wicked act he had performed. He remained under constant observation whilst awaiting the date, people not wanting him to have the satisfaction, if it can be termed that way, of ending his own life.

It was the State Senator who, on this occasion, oversaw the execution. Once more, Frank was offered his last request and, just as on the previous occasion, his choice was the perfectly simple, 'a banana please, Sir'.

These words were offered to the Prison Governor, but with the State Governor in attendance. The latter was not such an empathetic soul. This was, perhaps, because this whole horrific scene had played out for a second time while he was in office. He took it personally. Even if he had chosen not to, the public and press seemed to find cause to hold him partly responsible. He was going to ensure that 'Frankenstein' would die. Of that, neither he, the Prison Governor, nor Frank had the slightest doubt.

When it arrived, Frank slowly peeled the banana skin away from its fruit and in precisely seven mouthfuls the banana was eaten. He nodded his reply in response to whether he was ready. The prison chaplain was then allowed to enter and share prayers with Frank. Frank was not by nature a God-fearing man; he did believe in some higher benevolent power but as to who or what it was he could not really say. But he did pray and, it is told, that his prayers were focused upon Jean and the two young girls. I should have said, although I did take it for granted that you would understand that, just as was the case for the media at the time, I am not allowed to reveal their names.

Frank moved slowly but with a grim determination, towards his fate. He was strapped in and the skull cap attached with the hood being the last thing to be placed on him. His world was darkness which was soon to be perpetual. Everyone left the room.

At the flick of a rather large switch, the lights in the whole of the prison building dimmed and a humming sound could be heard. In the viewing gallery the State Governor allowed a slight smile to play upon his lips. He stared at Frank's contorted body as the current twisted him into a seemingly unnatural shape. The temperature where they were felt as it if had risen a few degrees. The sweat which could be seen dampening Frank's dark blue prison standard overalls was also forming on those who were watching the event. The 30 seconds seemed to endure for so much longer. At length, the lights flickered back to life and the humming ceased. No-one seemed to know what to do next. That is until the State Governor indicated the current should be shot through the slumped figure in the chair for a further 15 seconds. This was duly done and it was with a sense of grim satisfaction that the State Governor gave the signal for it to cease.

As they made their way to the small chamber where Frank was strapped to the chair, it was noticeably warmer. Upon opening the door the smell of burning rebelled in their nostrils and the same man who had smiled but a few minutes earlier now looked nauseous. The State Executioner reached the chair first; in truth none of the rest of the party was in any mind to get there ahead of him. Frank was slowly released from the bindings. It was as the skull cap was being detached, the hood having been removed to reveal an ashen grey face, like a steak which has gone to decay, that there was a sense that something was amiss. Whilst not revealed at the time, it is now widely accepted that the scream which rent the air came from the throat of the State Governor, although each of those unfortunate witnesses may equally have lain claim to such a reaction. It came as a result of the twitching neck muscles and a swollen tongue which slowly protruded from between Frank's lifeless lips. Slowly, ever so slowly, his nostrils flared which acted as a precursor to Frank opening his left eyelid. His sight duly followed. The experience left him unable to speak but he was capable of a rather dry, guttural choking sound. While no words could be said, he was alive. The two blasts of 200,000 volts of electricity had failed to see off Frank.

No-one knew what to do, but with three of the representatives of the nation's media in the viewing room, the team within the chamber had to accept the scarcely credible fact that Frank had cheated death. Again.

How Frank was smuggled from the prison and where he stayed over the two years that followed is unclear. Rumour has it that he found a number of sanctuaries in the homes of tram travellers who had known him in both the West and East Quarters. I can give you no more than that. Perhaps it was the competitive nature of the era, or perhaps the tentacles of the media did not stretch as far as we know to be the case today? Whatever the answer, he became invisible to the outside world. And oh that it would have remained that way, but Frank's tragic tale of torment and terror had another twist.

The Northern Quarter of the City was, and still is, the quieter, less thrusting counterpart of its more cosmopolitan siblings. If it were to happen anywhere it could only have been here. A new recruit to the company, adorned in the crimson and charcoal grey uniform, alighted the tram for his first day at work travlling the number 24 route. It was his first day here, but this man had travelled many a tram journey before, collecting fares and issuing tickets. He had told tales, told jokes, sung songs, listened to the travellers' stories. He was born to the job… and he was back. Frank had secured the position. How he had achieved this was never revealed. So many questions were asked; so many answers sought; so many people and contributors were blamed. But, in truth, perhaps everyone could and should share some small part of the blame. What sort of society can permit, even seemingly unknowingly, a convicted killer, on two separate occasions, to return to the very position from which he perpetuated his heinous acts? There is no answer other than the one which makes us all turn away from the uncomfortable thought that everyone has played their part in the tale.

Days moved into weeks. The weeks became months which, in their turn built into years. Five to be exact. Frank built a rapport with his audience, for, in truth, that is how he saw them and how they viewed themselves. They loved him and he, in turn, displayed a very genuine and deep affection for each and every one of them. Whilst each of his audience was an individual and very important in Frank's eyes, he would (and later did) confess that his namesake, Frank Senior, held that tiny but more special feeling in the tram company employee's heart. Frank Senior was almost an octogenarian and a decorated veteran from the First World War. The young Frank would listen intently to what the elder told him. He opened up to Frank in a way he had never spoken to anyone before. He spoke quietly and humbly and it had a profound effect upon his listener.

So how could it be that on the day of a veterans' parade, when in full ceremonial uniform and leaning heavily upon his walking stick, that Frank Junior acted in the way he did? As his older companion held his arm as the tram neared its stop, his guide and confidante kicked away that stick and pushed the older man from the tram and straight to his doom.

The screaming and crying which ensued was only drowned out by the wailing of the squad cars' sirens as they responded to the emergency call. You can imagine what then happened as it had already happened on two other occasions. However, this time Frank was taken to a different prison; away from the city itself, a place which incarcerated only the notorious. Had this played out a couple of years later, then the trial would have been televised, or at least part of it, but these days were still just over the horizon.

Frank listened to the court proceedings with a humble sense of déjà vu. He had done something very bad indeed; he didn't know exactly what, but the events that were relayed left him in no doubt. He stared morosely at the floor and wept bitterly.

Sentence was passed. The electric chair within the institution which he was imprisoned had capacity to transfer a current of 500,000 volts to the unfortunate person who would be enthroned upon it. And this was what was decreed. The President himself took a personal interest in the case and was represented at the execution by the Vice-President. Such a response was unheard of; Frank had become an image, a representative of something which haunted and shamed the nation and its people.

The viewing room had capacity for a dozen people. Selected media were given permission to record the proceedings. We should be thankful (if that is the right word to use) as it is their collective recollections of that evening which shape the conclusion to Frank's story. Shaven-headed and heavily shackled (although he had never, on any occasion, given rise to the belief that he would try to escape or try to injure anyone else. This was, and still is accepted.) Frank sat forlorn in his cell, awaiting his final call.

The door opened and the Prison Governor alongside the Chaplain and the jailer entered the room. Frank lifted his head and smiled weakly. It was returned, if not by the jailer who chose to turn his back on the proceedings.

"Frank, the chaplain will pray with you," said the Governor in a soft and calm voice. But before he does, I wish to offer you a last request."

Frank continued smiling and quietly made his choice the same as he had on two previous occasion,. "A banana, please."

It duly arrived and was consumed in a slow and, arguably, thoughtful manner. For a full 40 minutes the Chaplain and Frank prayed. And, as before, very rarely did these thoughts or prayers focus on his own well-being, but they were offered for those who had fallen victim at his hands and further families and friends. It was said that some of these people were in the very large crowd which had gathered outside the prison walls.

Once his communion with God, were he listening, was over, Frank was led very slowly to the larger chair which dominated the chamber which was to be his final destination. Strapped in, wired up and head covered, all others exited the room.

Once back in the viewing room, and with an expectant company alongside, the Prison Governor gave the nod for the current to be sent through Frank. The noise was deafening; the lights went out in the chamber and in the viewing room. Indeed, it was accepted that they flickered and fell on the blocks closest to the prison. It should also be said that these blocks were far from close to the centre of this episode. The current was for a full minute. The crackling noise and acrid smell permeated the room and two very hard-bitten journalists succumbed to their feeling of nausea.

When the lights finally came back on, all eyes were focused upon the lifeless body which seemed to have melded to the chair in which it had been seated. It took a full further five minutes before the straps were removed. No movement came from the body. The hood was removed. The skull cap, which held the electrodes, was detached from Frank's bare head, the white grey colour of his skin, damp with a sickly gleam of sweat. Frank remained still. The Vice President, for he had gone into the chamber, the Prison Governor and the executioner stood in silence. They looked at one another, not knowing what they should say.

It was the Vice President, out of the corner of his left eye, who caught the motion in the gallery. They were pointing and with a gradual realisation and sickening feeling he turned his head to see Frank begin to shudder. The Vice-President grabbed onto both of his companions and they slowly recoiled from the spectacle unfolding in front of them. But they couldn't escape it. It had to be confronted. The Prison Governor was the first to actually respond and find his voice. He approached and saw that Frank, eyes opening and lips moving was trying to speak. His mouth, tongue, throat and skin were, quite literally, parched. He needed water if they were to hear what he could tell them. The executioner left the room, glad to be out of there if only as a temporary reprieve. When he returned, he was still shaking but enough water remained within the jug and beaker he was carrying. The vessel was lifted to Frank's lips and he sipped and sipped. A full 10 minutes played out this scene and it was during this time that the Vice President felt emotions other than horror return to him. He was angry. How could this happen? Why didn't this monstrous aberration of a man die? How did he live to mock his executioners; the judicial system; his victims; society as a whole?

He stammered. "How? How can you.....how?" And then he thought he understood. "It's that banana isn't it?" he cried in a twisted form of euphoria.

Frank slowly lifted his head and slowly, very slowly, shook it from side to side to deny the Vice President's assertion.

"Then tell us. For the love of God and everything that is decent. How can you survive the death penalty on three occasions. You have had 500,000 volts surging through you for a full minute today. How is it possible? What are you?" the desperation was clear in his voice and his pleading was evident to all, none more so than Frank himself.

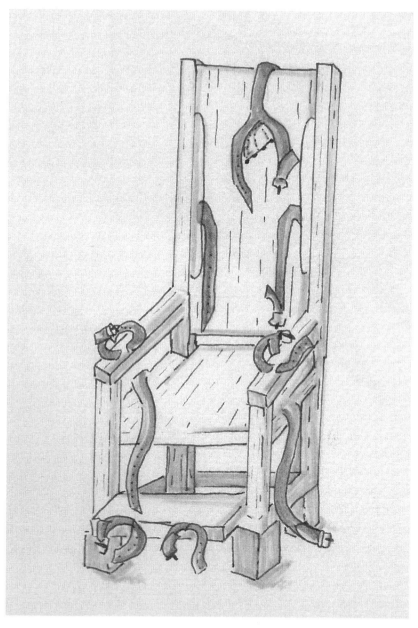

Frank looked up and on hearing the cry of the word 'how?' for the fourth time he replied ever so quietly: "The thing is, I'm a bad conductor."

THE MAGIC VIOLIN

Music can calm and soothe. It can restore people's faith in the world. It can bring people together. In some cases, it has the ability to build bridges and to make people forget previous grievances and ills; healing wounds and making people see the error of their ways.

This tale tells of just one of these instances. In truth, it is a scarcely believable story in which the heroine, possessed only of an elderly violin, was able to charm and pacify any who heard her play. It is a truly beautiful account of how one person, a totally unprepossessing and lonely soul, brought the natural kingdom together and achieved a serenity and harmony never known before. But I get ahead of myself.

The year was 1982 and Clarice was returning from work at a little past five o'clock on a Friday evening. There was nothing particularly special in this fact; indeed, it was almost exactly the same as it had been for the past five and half years. Prior to that, she had frequently been met by her late husband Richie every Friday and they had gone out together to enjoy the start of the weekend. Clarice didn't enjoy weekends anymore. Richie had died on a Wednesday morning on his way to work; the victim of a tragic accident when an elderly man lost control of his car as he suffered a heart attack. It is believed he was dead before his car mounted the pavement and struck Richie from behind. He died at the scene and Clarice was not aware until two Metropolitan police officers arrived at her place of work, mid-morning to turn off the light in her world. And that light had never flickered again; Richie and she were devoted to one another. Clarice took a period of compassionate leave, extended by a further two weeks, as the medical practice where she worked as a receptionist showed great empathy and helped her secure the gentlest return to her position that could have been offered to anyone in such unfortunate circumstances.

Five and a half years later, Clarice still worked at the practice and would probably still be doing so for years to come. Richie and she had no children: they weren't blessed with any is how Clarice spoke of this sadness. And so she alighted the bus at the same stop as always, a mere eight minute steady-paced walk to her small terraced, two bedroom cottage in a quieter part of an outer London suburb. She had to pass a parade of shops: launderette, newsagent-cum-convenience store; a Barnardo's charity store; a recently opened (and very good, by all accounts) Italian delicatessen which also had three small tables placed on the wide pavement outside its front offering cappuccino, espresso and that really tasty almond-based biscuit the name of which Clarice could never recall. Many were tempted and, although it was an early autumn evening, two of the tables were occupied. Clarice did frequent the establishment, but only really on a Saturday and nearly always in the late morning. There were also four tables inside and this is where she preferred to be. She wanted to keep herself to herself; to be anonymous.

Passing this row of establishments, Clarice went underneath the railway bridge which saw trains enter Victoria in a further 13 minutes, if not one of those stopping at the many stations between where she lived and the very busy London terminus. As Clarice came out from under the bridge's protection, immediately to her left on her side of the road was a shop which always caught her attention.

"Maurice's All Of Our Yesterdays."

The name used to make her cringe a little, but now she found its familiarity, and the poignancy it brought to her, comforting. 'Bric-a-brac' was far too tacky a term but it could not be called an antique shop. Its layout was, in truth, closer to a junk shop or a second-hand items shop, although much of what was inside may well have gone through many hands. Whilst not having any discernible plan to its layout, it wasn't untidy. Maurice's premises felt considered, it was just not quite possible to decide exactly what Maurice had been considering when he happened upon the floor plan. And Clarice liked it that way. She would also stop every day to look in the two windows. Rarely did she enter, but on occasions she did. And on a few of those occasions she had purchased an item; an ornate mantlepiece clock, three glazed terracotta pots which caught the eye on the short path to her front door, each having carefully tended, colourful shrubs which, in late spring and throughout the summer, offered powerful and enticing scents. Her other more recent purchase she could not recall as she stood outside the main window. No matter how she tried, it evaded her. "Not to worry; it'll come back to me," she resolved.

It was at this exact time that something caught her eye. A violin. Clarice had been a violinist of no small repute when a young girl and young lady. But Clarice was now 48 years old. She hadn't played for many a year. Somewhere at her home there was an old, rather damaged-beyond-repair musical instrument. In the attic, perhaps? All Clarice knew is that while it held sentimental and emotional value only; its days of producing soaring melodies had long gone. 'But could the same be said for me?' thought Clarice.

Without consciously making the decision, she found herself inside the shop and beginning a conversation with Mr Frampton who, within a couple of minutes, insisted Clarice call him Maurice.

In truth, a similar opening conversation had occurred on a few

125

times over the years. Clarice smiled at the thought and then ventured, to enquire about the violin. "Ah, yes," replied Maurice. "A very interesting instrument. I held it in my possession for a great many years, on and off," he added. Seeing the look of curiosity appear on her face, it was Maurice's turn to smile. "I have sold it on three previous occasions, each time it has been returned to me, directly or indirectly. It seems to serve a purpose for the purchaser and, once achieved, it finds its resting place back here. Strange, really," Maurice seemed to drift in memories, his kind, old face showing a happy, yet wistful, look.

Clarice listened politely. Clarice was always polite. She had warmed to Maurice on the first occasion they spoke and, now she was reacquainted, she felt no different whatsoever. She did, though, think his tale to be ever so slightly romanticised.

"Would you like to have a closer look?" asked Maurice and without waiting for a reply he manoeuvred himself between some precariously placed crockery, lamps and old golf clubs, of all things, to reach the violin.

"Do you play?" he ventured.

"Oh, a long time ago," blushed Clarice. "And strictly as an amateur;" she continued, her natural modesty preventing her from adding any further comment as to her level of capability.

As soon as she held the rather scratched violin it seemed to feel warm. Looking back later that evening she would think that it seemed to mould to her. Yet at the same time she would also giggle a little at seemingly being guilty of the same romanticism she had discerned in Maurice. The bow felt equally at home in her right hand, as if she had played only the day before, not that three decades had passed. As she passed the bow over the strings, she was amazed that the violin sounded almost perfectly tuned; a very quick and minor adjustment and it was ready to be played.

Maurice nodded and smiled, once again. "It sounds like you've found a friend," he said. Clarice could only agree, but the £50.00 price was far more than she would have chosen to spend on anything simply for her own pleasure. Maurice seemed to read her thoughts and added, "Why don't you take it for the weekend and see what you think? Play it at home and find out if it does belong to you. No charge and no commitment. If you decide against purchasing, then you simply need to return it to me."

Clarice immediately said she couldn't accept such a kind and generous arrangement but Maurice would hear no more and steadfastly refused to accept any form of deposit or guarantee which Clarice offered. Eventually, she agreed. She could feel a frisson of excitement as she watched Maurice place the violin in its old case, likewise the bow, and hand both to her. "Enjoy, Clarice," he added and bade her farewell. It wasn't until she arrived at her front gate that she realised she hadn't actually told Maurice her name. She was sure. Perhaps she had on a previous occasion? If so, then Maurice had an exceptionally good memory.

As she dwelt on this thought she seemed to sense a warmth emanating from the violin case. She had to take it out, there and then. Forcing herself to step into her small front garden and close the gate behind her, she immediately began to play. The melody soared; it was as if she hadn't had a 30-year interlude. As she played, the dog which stayed behind the gate of the house opposite hers ceased its barking (it always barked when people passed by, on either side of the road). Looking across as she played, she could see that the boisterous boxer had sat with its head inclined towards its right shoulder and was, it seemed, looking at her in a state of complete calm. Awakening to her situation, Clarice stopped playing, shivered a little – but this was a tremor of excitement – and quickly hurried through her front door. Before she closed it she glanced across the road to see the boxer still sat, head on one side, as if in a trance. Strange, thought Clarice. As she ate her supper, slightly earlier than was normally the case, it wasn't with the customary sense of being alone for she could not leave thoughts of the violin which sat, with its bow, on the armchair next to her. Richie's chair she still thought… and always will. Just what was it about this violin? The image of the dog over the road would not leave her and it was whilst contemplating the boxer's expression that her train of thought was interrupted by the ear-splitting screech that rent the air. To say Clarice was startled would be an understatement but, once she gathered herself, she moved quickly to her kitchen, opened the door to be met with the sight of two large tomcats sizing each other up, hissing and spitting their fury. Clarice waving her arms and shouting at them had not the slightest effect; their eyes were locked on each other and they were oblivious to anything and everything else.

Clarice stopped her gesticulations, turned on her heel and returned promptly holding the violin and bow. Without hesitation, she started to play and as soon as the melody met the air, both feline fiends broke their fixed gaze on each other and transferred their attention to the person playing such wonderful music. Within moments their body language had changed completely; the ginger and white cat padding forward and sitting next to his jet-black former adversary. Both inclined their heads, ever so slightly to the right and half-closed their eyes as they appeared to enter a state of total calm and relaxation. Clarice continued to play, a feeling of euphoria swelling her very being. And as she played, the birds which had perched at a very safe distance whilst the two cats had faced off, chose to flutter down to her lawn and onto her fence or washing line until she could see over 30 and of different types. The birds, too, sat with their heads resting slightly to the side and remained still and silent. They showed no concern or alarm to be in the presence of the cats who, in turn, simply sat listening to the beautiful music. A hedgehog scuttled from beneath the large gorse bush close to Clarice. It, too, stopped busying itself and sat, focusing upon the violinist. And as she played, she noticed three frogs leap out of her small pond and come to stop next to the ginger and white cat. The surface of the pond bubbled up as Clarice's ornamental goldfish broke the water and did their best to become part of the audience which was appreciating the early evening rendition.

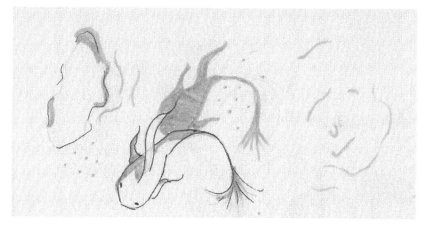

When, eventually, Clarice stopped playing, she surveyed her audience. They remained there, quiet, still, charmed and only, very slowly, did they move. But in so doing, they displayed undue deference to their neighbours, each moving with a serenity that would not be broken. The music of the violin had, it seemed, united the various creatures; natural competitors and predators had ceased their normal behaviour. A harmonious air had settled upon them all and at its centre was Clarice with the very special violin.

To say that Clarice was excited would do her state of being no justice whatsoever. She did not sleep until the early hours; she was convinced that Mr Maurice Frampton's description of the violin was no romanticism. If anything, she thought, he had been restrained. And he had allowed her to take it home and to play it. She then recalled that its previous owners had either returned it or it had found its way back to him. And then the thought struck her but, in truth, it had been in her subconscious mind ever since her experience in her back garden. "I'm meant to have this violin. It is an opportunity. I have been given a purpose," she reasoned. And from there her purpose quickly took shape. The animals had been becalmed. A feeling of peace and contentment had been brought to creatures who were distressed or angry.

If this could be achieved on creatures who were pets or who lived in a suburban setting, could the same be achieved with creatures who were not domesticated and didn't live in such a a setting? Her mind raced. What could she do? What *should* she do? She had to find out if the violin could weave its magic elsewhere. And then she struck upon a plan; she would visit the zoo the very next day and very early so as to be one of the first visitors. Whilst still excited, her plan gave way to immeasurable images of peace and calm amongst the zoo's inhabitants and it was during such images that sleep crept up on her and she tumbled into a very deep and satisfying rest.

Her resolve was such that Clarice was wide awake and feeling totally refreshed despite having not had quite five hours' sleep. She hadn't set her alarm and so was relieved to see the time being shortly before 7am. Three quarters of an hour to get ready and she would be striding purposefully to catch the No 46 bus which would meander its way to the road which lay adjacent to the one which held the entrance to the zoo. And so it was that Clarice was clutching her violin on the seat nearest to the front of the lower deck of the No 46. Interestingly, that is how she now thought of it; this was not just a violin it was *her* violin. Thanking the driver, Clarice stepped down onto the pavement and immediately strode to the entrance of the zoo. She was pleased to see that there was little by way of a crowd, despite the opening time being a mere twenty minutes' away. These minutes dragged and Clarice tried to occupy herself and not look too conspicuous. Not only was she, it seemed, the only solo visitor but she was, most definitely, the only visitor carrying a violin. To avoid the staring and pointing of any indiscreet fellow visitors, she focused upon the creatures who would get to listen to her playing. This occupied the full waiting time and, as she received her ticket in exchange for her money, she determined to visit the penguins first of all, then the ape house and then either the giraffes or elephants.

Clarice hadn't been to the zoo for many, many years; indeed, she couldn't recall the last visit with any certainty. She had to rely on the many signs which directed excited visitors to their desired destination. It was of no surprise to Clarice that the penguins' marina was marked on the first signpost she encountered. "They're always really popular," she smiled. Without hesitation, she walked briskly to meet the penguins and, entering the marina, saw she was the first to arrive. She got her violin out of its case and, noticing the penguins were engaged in a variety of activities, she began to play. Their reaction was instantaneous: all heads turned towards her. Those swimming in the water came right forward, tapping their beaks on the transparent wall which separated the penguins from visitors. As they were unable to stay still at this particular place they, as one, decided to swim swiftly back to the nearest rock surface and join those already massed there to enjoy Clarice's playing. In no time whatsoever, every single penguin was sat on its haunches, head leant slightly to the right, concentrating intently upon the beautiful melody which floated around their compound. Clarice wanted to stay and play, so happy was she on seeing their sense of rapture. However, she had a plan and she needed to stick to it. Bringing her playing to a somewhat abrupt, if still musically sound, ending, she hurried out the way she had entered.

Next was the ape house. This was going to be more difficult for, as she suspected, she wasn't alone. Another five families were looking at the gorillas and baboons. But Clarice had prepared for just such an eventuality. Taking her violin out, she coughed gently, gained the others' attention and proceeded to explain that she was a professor at the university and was conducting an experiment to see the effect certain music and musical instruments had upon caged animals. It couldn't be argued that her first assertion was totally untrue, but what she claimed to be doing, was true. "Just a fib," Clarice told herself, "and it is for the greater good." As she began to play, Clarice marvelled at how bold she had become in such a short period of time. Was she really the same quiet introvert who had craved only privacy and her own company?

The gorillas, who had shown no interest in the visitors up to this point, looked up and opened their eyes wide in acknowledgement of what they were hearing. The family of baboons, as Clarice presumed they were, ceased their bickering and turned to find out the source of the music. Each primate sat down, facing Clarice, head inclined to the right and keeping absolutely still. The gorillas and baboons were in separate rooms with a solid, opaque wall in between. As Clarice glanced up, she could see that their response mirrored the others' reactions. Clarice was thrilled and continued playing for a further five minutes. And it was during this period of time that she suddenly became aware that the people had diverted their attention towards her, away from the gorillas and baboons. And they were still, even the excitable young children. They were silent too, including the two infants who were in pushchairs. A look of contentment was shared among them and the blissful gaze followed Clarice as she smiled and nodded farewell before exiting.

"It's true! It really is!" she couldn't contain her excitement. But, elated as she was, Clarice knew that her time at the zoo was limited. Word would spread and she wouldn't have the freedom to play to the animals. She would have to forgo the giraffes and elephants. Accepting this, she made for the exit, only to realise that she was passing a building which housed butterflies. Clarice hadn't considered such creatures before in relation to the music but she did love their delicate beauty. She suspected that the Butterfly House would not have any visitors at this time in the morning. She was wrong: other people were in the spacious building - an elderly couple and a family with a boy and girl of primary school ages, Clarice reasoned. On this occasion she chose not to introduce her intentions and simply began playing.

The air, which had been thick with the fluttering of wings and a kaleidoscope of colours seemed to clear and became bright and still. Every single butterfly had ceased its individual flight and alighted on the many branches available. Their wings were closed momentarily before opening to display their resplendent colours. They stayed in such a position giving the impression to all there that they were peacefully enjoying the beautiful melody that now filled their air. Clarice stayed playing for a full 10 minutes more, her fellow visitors remained in motionless reverie throughout. Five further visitors also joined them during this time, entering the house as if it were a place of worship, respectfully standing still, paying attention to the music, looking at Clarice and the butterflies which were perched all around her.

Without any fuss or attention, she slowed her playing and quietly retreated from the Butterfly House and made her way out of the zoo. Once back on the No 46 bus home, she looked at the violin case which lay across her lap. She tried, but simply couldn't fully contemplate the power which resided within.

It was as she was savouring her evening meal later that one final thought entered Clarice's head.

"I've seen the response of creatures who were pets, creatures who live in suburbia and creatures who have, to an extent, been tamed by being in a man-made dwelling. But what about the wild? The true wild? Would it be the same? *Could* it be the same? Clarice thought further and it was over her plate of fish and salad that an idea began to form in her mind.

In many ways, the wild and the thought of 'safari' shocked and scared Clarice. It was absolutely certain that the contemplation of going on a safari holiday would never, ever have entered her mind prior to being united with the violin. But Clarice had grown in confidence and spirit. She resolved to think about it the following day, Sunday, and then she would act on her decision. Secretly, she had already made up her mind and she knew that on Monday she would need to pay two visits. The first would be to the travel agent to organise the 'holiday of a lifetime' and the second would be to pay Mr Frampton the £50.00 she now owed him. Whilst thinking this, Clarice also realised that she would have to ask for holiday from the medical practice.

"So, that's three visits then," she said, quietly, to herself.

Clarice was no longer surprised at how quickly she put her plan into action. She had, in such a short space of time, became a determined and focused lady. She secured an 18-day break from the medical practice and was pleasantly surprised that it started the next Saturday. She had been very fortunate that neither of her contemporaries in the practice had booked a break for the next

135

few weeks. She could go. All she needed now was to secure that break.

The travel agent's window boasted many foreign adventures as Clarice stepped outside during her lunch break. None offered details for safari though. Notwithstanding, Clarice entered, sat down in front of Matthew and explained her wish. Matthew raised an eyebrow; he clearly didn't picture Clarice as an adventure-seeker, but his customer relations manner was very good and he immediately got down to researching her request and putting together the 'holiday of a lifetime' for Clarice. Now, please remember, this was before the days of the internet and putting together a holiday courtesy of the click of a keyboard was well in the future. Matthew had many phone calls to make. He explained this to Clarice and they agreed she would return the following day at the same time. Clarice expressed her gratitude and took her leave.

As she entered 'All Of Our Yesterdays' shortly after 5pm, she already held five £10 notes in her hand. Mr Frampton, Maurice, smiled as he was handed the note and politely enquired as to how she felt about the violin.

Clarice was cautious in her reply whilst also showing her enthusiasm.

"It is just right for me. It sounds so beautiful; it makes my playing so much clearer and purer than I remember it being," she replied.

"The violin has its own way of finding the person who needs it the most," said Maurice. "I genuinely believe that. I am very happy for you Clarice."

On this occasion Clarice didn't feel Maurice's words were, in any way, a romanticism of her situation. She was inclined to agree. She did, however, keep her experiences to herself; the time would come when she would share what was happening. Clarice smiled broadly, bade Maurice farewell and exited his emporium to take the short walk home.

The violin sat in its case, on her kitchen table. Whilst waiting for it to be time to have her supper, Clarice took out the instrument and played it in her back garden. As the melody floated on the air, all the noises in her own and the neighbouring gardens ceased. Slowly, cats, birds and a lone Jack Russell dog gathered close to her. As she had been accustomed to seeing, they formed a silent, attentive audience, heads inclined to their right and gently musing on the melody. Clarice played for far longer than she had intended and it was with more than a little reluctance that she drew her playing to a close. She smiled at the menagerie gathered in front of her, before realising where she was and closing her door behind her. Very slowly and very calmly, her audience dispersed, respectful of one another. The hours seemed to stretch out before Clarice and she found the following morning to last an inordinate amount of time before she could resume her discussions with Matthew.

On entering the travel agent on the High Street, Clarice was instantly reassured by the welcoming smile on Matthew's face. The conversation seemed to fly and while Matthew understandably undertook the lead and did the vast majority of the talking, Clarice sat nodding her agreement.

By the time she left, Clarice had purchased a safari holiday for a sum of money much greater than she had ever spent on a holiday before in her life. She was travelling to Cape Town, South Africa and from there would be part of a group of 12 other adventurers, spending nights at three different lodges. Being a solo traveller, she did have to pay the obligatory supplements. Momentarily, this made Clarice very sad; she would have loved to have been going with Richie. But the spirit of the violin and the harmony and fellowship it gave seemed to have brought Richie back to her in a certain way. Her sadness passed as she nodded to herself in believing that Richie was with her and would be on the safari.

The intervening days didn't drag, somewhat surprisingly, as Clarice spent her time packing and checking that she possessed everything she needed to ensure her wellbeing and potential enjoyment.

Clarice managed to keep the violin and bow as part of her hand luggage. It was safely stored above her head and Clarice relaxed, dozing off as the plane made its journey towards a different continent.

Upon landing, Clarice was really happy to experience a smooth transfer and to find the mini coach which was to ferry them to their first destination waiting for her and her fellow travellers as they exited the airport. The transit journey took almost four hours but the mini coach was very comfortable and its air conditioning kept the excited travellers cool and calm.

Clarice chose to keep her own company at the start of her holiday. She didn't want to explain the presence of her violin any more than she needed to. She simply explained: "It reassures me and I always play it sometime during a day… But please do not worry, it will be quiet and will not intrude upon you." Her reassurance seemed to satisfy her listeners and its presence was not mentioned again. The lodge did not disappoint with a spacious, air-conditioned bedroom, a powerful, refreshing shower and a large bath. The downstairs offered an open roaring fire which heated a high vaulted lounge area which also contained the dining table. Meals were prepared by a resident chef whose creations tasted better than anything Clarice had ever eaten before. She was going to be happy. No, she *was* happy.

Nonetheless, she did not lose sight of her reason for being there and Clarice was impatient to be 'in the wild'. However, it soon became clear that this was going to be far from easy to achieve. They were accompanied everywhere once they left the lodge. Three days passed with early rises and late returns. They experienced the sight of elephants drinking from a water hole; giraffes and zebras feeding contentedly without sign of any predator. On the third day it was the turn of the lions; in the afternoon heat they seemed somewhat indolent, fatigued by the heat and not stressed even as the three jeeps ferried the sightseers within close proximity.

Clarice marvelled at these creatures, but despite being so captivated, the thought of what their response to her music would be did not leave her. The feeling became stronger on the drive back. They were arriving at their second lodge, their luggage having been transferred for them whilst they had been lion-gazing.

Upon arrival, they were given a mere 30 minutes to freshen up and meet in the foyer. They were to eat in the bush. And so it passed that the band of travellers were given an armed escort as they walked no more than 15 minutes to seat themselves around a campfire. The most succulent barbecue was to follow; all played out to the sounds of the wild. Never a roar or a growl, but the occasional 'whoop' or screech alongside the constant chattering sounds that never left the air. It was a quite amazing experience.

The pathway to the firepit was very well trodden and led straight back to the lodge. People were tired and no one accepted the offer of a nightcap. This suited Clarice as she had already worked out what she was going to do. She was going to return to the firepit once everyone was asleep! She realised that she was breaking the most basic rule that had been stressed to them on a number of occasions, that at no time should they ever venture out of the lodge unaccompanied. She did feel guilty, but her need to speak to the animals and find that universal harmony was greater. She had to do it!

The two main locks on the solid front door took strength to release. It was even harder to achieve this feat whilst not making the kind of noise which would attract the attention of those within the building. Once achieved, Clarice stood on the threshold, drew in a very deep breath and stepped outside. With each step away from the lodge, she felt more alive. The sky was littered with stars which shone brightly and guided her forth seeming to assist her in her quest. In no time, she was back beside the smouldering embers of the firepit which still threw out great warmth, giving welcome to Clarice.

She stood, looked around her and listened to the noises in the vegetation. There were scurrying sounds and cries, quite close by, and she relished these sounds of the natural world in her ears.

Clarice took out her violin, lifted it to rest beneath her chin and raised her bow. Her fingers trembled in anticipation as, softly, she began to play.

The notes rose into the night air and floated away into the darkness. Within moments the chattering and scurrying ceased and, gradually, with caution at first, eyes blinked their presence to Clarice. With increasing boldness, yet still timid in step, their owners began to show themselves. Creatures of all shapes and sizes came forward to sit around the firepit which effectively formed an amphitheatre. The enclave offered a wonderful natural acoustic allowing Clarice's melodies to soar into the night welcoming each and every note.

Small creatures sat towards the front, the larger members of the congregation naturally affording them pride of place.

An astonishing array of God's creatures assembled in complete harmony and communion with one another, to listen to the sounds of the violin. The music spoke of love, contentment and peace. It showed the way that all could live alongside one another. There would be no more suffering.

Clarice continued to play. Larger animals, beasts of the wild, joined the throng, content to sit near the rear, overwhelmingly glad to be a part of the assembly. The antelope sat next to the hyena; the rhinoceros rubbed shoulders with the jaguar; elephants made way for small, furry creatures which Clarice could not name. The zebras lay down in a position most like the sphinx in Egypt, allowing the large snakes which had slithered into the arena to coil contentedly against their bodies. Spiders sat, cross-legged, near the front and each and every creature had tilted its head, ever so slightly to the right and wore upon its face the glazed expression of delirium. Each was able to share in the joy of togetherness. In the trees, birds of many sizes whose plumage was rich in its perfection, perched silently, heads to the right as they, too, joined in this great communion.

The bow now flashed across the strings as the melody increased its pace whilst never losing its charm and comfort to the listeners. Ever so gradually, its pace decreased until its speed and pitch leant it a poignancy. Far from sad, instead it sought to encourage all present to look inside themselves to reach deep to find what they could bring to this new union of nature.

As this solitary melody rang in their ears, a very distant sound could just be made out. It was deep and became increasingly louder, louder, even LOUDER until, with a smashing of foliage, a mighty lion leapt into the massed audience, scattering the silent worshippers wide. With two bounds, it cleared the remaining creatures and opening its mighty jaws and baring its knife-like teeth it severed Clarice's head, shoulders and arms from her body, crushing and splintering the violin in the same movement. It chewed and tore apart her lifeless body, the rich red wave of her blood flowing freely from its mouth and coursing from her torso. The animals sat, horrified and in silence; stunned by what they had witnessed.

After what seemed an eternity, one of the giraffes ventured forward and with a look of abject misery and a look of total incomprehension and asked, in a very quiet voice, "Why? Why? How could you? Couldn't you hear the beauty of the music? Couldn't you understand the joy and peace of its message?" Tears were streaming down its cheeks as the words were uttered.

The lion looked up, surprised it was being addressed. Raising its left paw in a rather theatrical fashion, it cupped its ear and asked 'Eh?'

IF MUSIC BE THE FOOD OF ACTION HEROES...

I'm not too sure that William Shakespeare, the Bard, would normally be associated with such cinematic legends as Sylvester Stallone, Bruce Willis and Arnold Schwarzenegger. He wasn't renowned for his action blockbusters, although I suppose it could be argued that some of his tragedies saw violence meted out and an increasing body count which would rival the output of our three heroes.

However, our tale starts very far away from the silver screen and finds the intrepid three in a state of collective misery. The year is 1999, it is December and the new millennium is fast approaching. But it brings them no joy. For, you see, their joint commercial enterprise, Planet Hollywood - the upmarket burger restaurant themed around the movies - has just gone bust. Only two years earlier, it had been a thriving enterprise but, as can so often happen, over-expansion led to vulnerabilities. As its popularity waned, its debts began to mount and, despite efforts to downsize and reinvent itself, the chain collapsed.

It is a Friday night at a bar in the foothills of Beverley Hills and the three action stars are met together to drown their sorrows. We find them hunched over a table in a slightly dark corner of the room. Music plays in the background, a plaintive voice is reflecting on the end of his relationship and asking, in a rhetorical manner, just what he could have done differently. Heads are covered, faces downcast and eyes focusing only upon the drinks in front of them. The scene of broken manhood brings nothing but despair; they are a picture of dejection and misery. The outsider who triumphed so spectacularly against all odds, who they were so used to playing, was nowhere to be seen. Not one word or gesture of defiance was evident.

Eventually, Sly Stallone raised his head and took a long look at his friends. His lugubrious features moved slowly before he uttered the words, "What are we gonna do? How are we gonna turn this around?" His eyes moved, even more slowly than before, as he surveyed his friends' reactions. Neither spoke, nor moved. After what seemed an incredibly long silence, Bruce Willis simply shrugged his shoulders and followed this with a slow shake of his head. Arnie looked up and in his deadpan, stonewall delivery said, "Nothing to be done." Silence returned. No words seemed to be exchanged as the waitress approached with three fresh drinks and collected the empty glasses. Only Stallone looked up in acknowledgement and nodded their collective thanks to her. They drank slowly, conversing little and continued to look defeated. It was Stallone, again, who broke the silence.

"Guys. We gotta do something. We can't just sit and drink this away. We're action heroes; we laugh at danger. We're not gonna get beaten on this one. Are we understood?"

His last comment was more rhetorical and that was probably just as well, he reflected, as Bruce and Arnie barely mumbled their assent.

"Come on!" he suddenly yelled. "We're gonna do this. Right? Right!" he bellowed. The few other customers in the bar looked up, as one, and stared, with a look of concern on their faces, in the friends' direction. The notable rise in decibels had its desired effect on his drinking companions, who looked at him, in some state of alarm, before vigorously adding their agreement. "Good. That's that sorted," Stallone replied. "I've got an idea that might just work, but I need to get back and do a bit of research. You guys, you have a think and see if you can come up with anything and we'll meet back here tomorrow evening at 20 hundred hours."

Without waiting for a reply, he drained his beer, got up, pushed back his bar stool and strode from the table exiting the door without looking back.

Bruce and Arnie looked at each other and, at the same time, shook their heads before returning to their silent companionship, slowly drawing on their beers. But before long, Bruce sat back and announced.

"He's right, y'know. We can't take this lying down. We're gonna find something." He brought his fist down on the table to emphasise the strength of his recently acquired conviction. Arnie nodded, adding a defiant, "Yeah" before standing up, jerking his head at the door and encouraging Bruce to leave before ordering another beer.

The following evening, at 15 minutes before 8 o'clock, as he would refer to the time, a fidgeting Bruce Willis was sat at their table and was just about to start on his second beer. He was nervous, not only because of his predicament with respect to his share in the restaurant chain which was now in administration, but because he had completely failed to come up with a single idea that could extricate the three friends from their situation. He wasn't looking forward to the others arriving and having to admit that he'd come up with nothing. Then again, what if they'd got something that would pull them off the canvas and get them punching again? This raised his spirits, even though he realised his mind had slipped into a boxing analogy. "Boxing? Where did that come from?!" he wondered, but tried to seek reassurance that it may have been a sign that his friend, Sly 'Rocky Balboa' Stallone had struck gold with the idea he had hinted at the previous evening. As this thought played in his brain he became aware of a large and imposing figure coming towards him. It was Arnie. Looking up, the expectant smile on Bruce's face fell away in recognition of the strong, leaden look worn by his companion. In truth, this was pretty much how Arnie appeared at any given time, but the seriousness of their situation, allied to the fragility of his nervous state, made Bruce quick to accept the negative interpretation. He wasn't wrong.

"Nothing to be done," mumbled Arnie. "Nothing. I have stayed up all night and have spent the whole of today trying to think of how we can get out of this. Who can we turn to? I can think of nothing and no-one. We are finished." He slumped down at the table, looked straight at Bruce and offered a very slight shrug of this shoulders.

"Arnie," panicked Bruce. "Pull yourself together. You're indestructible: nothing beats you." But he could see that his rushed words of confidence and encouragement were having no effect whatsoever on the shadow, albeit a very large and solid shadow, of a man hunched opposite him.

"What are we gonna say to Sly?" he cried. "How can we tell him we're beat? Washed up? Dead in the water?" His tone became slightly hysterical and his mood was not improved when, on his final word, the figure of Stallone framed the doorway. As he made his way to the bar, Bruce hissed at Arnie.

"Who's gonna speak first? What are we gonna say to him?" Bruce realised that he sounded as if he were pleading.

"God! I've fallen this far!" he muttered. Footsteps approaching their table announced the arrival of Sylvester Stallone, bearing three bottles of beer and wearing an unusually broad smile on his haggard face. His appearance had an unnerving effect upon the other two. Was Sly genuinely happy? Had their collective misery and lowly status left him slightly unhinged? Bruce's thoughts were muddled. What should he say first?

"Nothing to be done!" was the decisive declaration from Arnie. That he was a man of few words could not be denied, but he chose to repeat those few words so soon after his initial announcement was no real surprise. It certainly got to the heart of the matter.

Bruce stammered his contribution. "Sly, we've tried. We've been round all the houses in our minds, no-one's been answering. Just closed doors!" He looked up at Stallone who simply put the beers on the table in front of them and reached out to place a reassuring hand on each of their shoulders.

"Guys, guys. Don't worry. I know how tough it feels but we're in this together. Yes?" Sylvester Stallone didn't wait for an answer; he knew they were and they'd get through this. And he knew this with absolute certainty because he had a plan. He sat down, took a pull from his bottle, leant back before continuing, "Here it is. We're action heroes. Agreed?" The other two looked at each other, the interest gathering as they nodded their agreement. "We inspire people; we take on the roles that pitch the outsiders against great odds, into some pretty damned hair-raising situations. And we win. We triumph. We smash those odds and do so with passion and energy." At this point, he glanced at Arnie, quickly reflected on what he'd just claimed and even more quickly, moved on.

"What's the movie-going world waiting for? It'll be a blockbuster involving all three of us," he enthused.

"Er, Sly," countered Bruce. "I think we'd got that far but we just couldn't think of what it would be. What's new, what's great for people to wanna come see us?" he bemoaned.

"Music," responded Stallone, the beam returning to his face.

"Music?" echoed Arnie, again keeping to his limited repertoire. Bruce adding, "But, Sly, we aren't musicians. We're actors. We're physical. Not musical." His tone had become defiant. If this was what Sly thought was going to save them, they were truly in one great mess!

"Woah! Hold on there guys. I know we ain't no musical gods, but we can play them; others can play the actual music."

"What sort of music?" enquired a disbelieving Bruce. "Rock, metal….. jazz," he pondered, hardly believing his own words.

"Nope," continued Stallone. "Classical!"

"Classical?!" Bruce and Arnie echoed this time, both unable, and unwilling, to keep their feeling of incredulity to themselves. For the third time the word 'classical' was spoken, as Sylvester Stallone went on to explain….

"Guys, those classical musicians are the action heroes of their time. They wowed their audiences; they were the superstars. Think of it… Beethoven. That guy wrote some of the most moving, passionate music the world knows and get this. For the large part of his composing life, he was one hundred percent stone deaf. Incredible. Just imagine it; writing beautiful tunes and not being able to hear them yourself? Man, the pathos. Just how tragic is that?

"And I know I can empathise with that." Bruce and Arnie listened in wide-eyed amazement: words failed them. Very strange in the case of Bruce; less so for Arnie.

150

"Just think of the terrible sadness and the pity I evoked in Rocky," Stallone continued. "That deep emotion, the feeling of loss and being beaten down but coming through in Rocky II and Rocky III. And IV and V. Man, I know I can bring this Beethoven guy, with his inner sadness, to life on the big screen!"

He leant back, looked up at the others for the first time and said "Whaddya think?"

Now during his recollection of great emotional range in the various Rocky incarnations, a feeling had struck Bruce. His initial dumbfounded state and mild horror had given way to a thought which was now flourishing.

"Hey, Sly, you may just have got it! Yeah, yeah. Think about it, Mozart. Wolfgang Amadeus Mozart. He was the wild man at court. He broke the rules; he was a maverick, the original bad man. Well, that's me, isn't it? Can't you see it?" he cried. "Sylvester Stallone nodded in agreement, offering enthusiastic encouragement. "You got it, Bruce!" Arnie seemed somewhat more circumspect; his strong look, as ever, betraying little emotion. Bruce was in full swing. "Just think of all those roles where I've been the wild man, the authority breaker, the guy who does it his way and to hell with the rest.... John McCain in Die Hard! And then there was Die Hard 2." He stopped, pausing briefly, to recall his back catalogue before adding, "And 3 and 4. This guy Mozart, well, he is me and I'm him." Bruce was a totally different man to the one who had begun listening to his friend's idea, open-mouthed and wanting to weep.

"You're there, Bruce!" cried Sylvester. Mozart is you! You're that loose cannon."

"And you're Beethoven to a tee," Bruce responded. "Stone deaf and not able to hear the gorgeous music he was writing. That is totally tragic. And you do tragic, Sly. No-one empathises quite like you."

They turned to Arnie. Stallone ventured, "What's it to be Arnie? Are you with us?"

Bruce joined him, "Yeah, come on. Arnie. This has wings. Who are you gonna be?"

Arnie placed his hands on the table, slowly turned his head from one to the other before announcing, "I'll be Bach."

SIR WALTER RETURNS
FROM THE COLD

When last we heard of the brave Sir Walter Raleigh, he was cradling the horrifically wounded body of his Ship's Boy who had just informed him that he had failed to locate the 'Long Lost Bacon Tree'. Now we are not party as to how he managed to navigate his way back to the shores of England. Nor are we party to the reception he was afforded nor, even, what thence transpired. However, what we do know is that, no more than five and no fewer than two years later, Sir Walter found himself in the foothills of the Himalayas. And he found himself alone. Snow-bound. With no food and no energy.

And here the story would undoubtedly have finished, making it very brief and of no great note, had it not been for the chance passing of a cluster of seven trappist monks who dwelt in the only habitation in the particular valley in which a snowblind Sir Walter had stumbled. Sir Walter would, gradually, learn how incredibly fortunate he had been to have been discovered by this benevolent band of brothers. Fate, which had seemed to have dealt so callously with him had, at the last, relented and granted him a road to a sanctuary and his eventual recuperation and redemption.

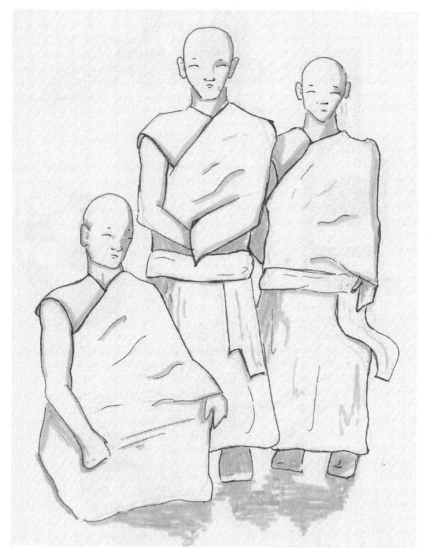

But let us take a very brief detour to explain why Sir Walter was where he was. In truth, his star had fallen somewhat with his failure to bring back the 'Long Lost Bacon Tree' to Queen Elizabeth. Her rather draconian pronouncement that Sir Walter would be beheaded should this have been the outcome, didn't occur. Clearly. She relented as she could tell how hard he had tried and the terrible fate that had befallen his crew. But it could not be denied that the epic quest had been a failure. A glorious one, perhaps, but a failure nonetheless. Sir Walter returned to being a 'courtier' given access to nearly everywhere within whichever royal palace was in vogue. Such privilege was granted only to the monarch's favoured few. Sir Walter was incredibly proud, incredibly grateful and, more than these, incredibly relieved. His execution had been revoked and he had, in effect, been given a gold-plated pension. Sir Walter relished this for a short period of time and then his incredible relief gave way to incredible boredom. He felt trapped and he detested the obsequious behaviour of his fellow courtiers and the inevitable, oh so important, politics which shaped and dictated every breathing moment at court. He couldn't deny it; he hated it! Something had to be done.

"I'm an explorer, an adventurer," he mused. "I explore. I take on adventures. I am meant to do these things and these things I shall continue to do!" he announced, a little too loudly, perhaps as these were his internal thoughts.

Looking around him and thanking his lucky stars that, for once, he did not have any of the faceless flunkies which fawned upon his every move nearby, he set to determining how he could embrace the nobility of a new challenge. And, more to the point, just what the challenge would be.

Now, dear reader, this I'm afraid is where the story becomes, albeit briefly, rather vague. That Sir Walter was next found, quite literally, in the foothills of the Himalayas is recorded fact. Surely he can't have been mountaineering, although the very area is home to climbs which beyond question, even today, are among the most challenging and treacherous known to the mountaineering fraternity. No oxygen tanks; compass; pickaxes… no equipment which is considered essential to attempt to scale such behemoths.

It seems more likely that he was trekking. There is no mention anywhere in the tale that tells of there being any fellow travellers. Perhaps he just took to, what was then and still is today, a remote and untamed area of our globe. Was he to report on his findings? Map the area? It is not known. What is known is that he was so close to certain death due to hypothermia that the monks who carried him back to their remote monastery took him straight to their chapel and, having wrapped him in furs, they prayed fervently for his soul's flight to heaven. His body, however, clearly wished for its soul to remain below for some time longer. Sir Walter did not pass on so he was then carried to what would, today, be described as their medical quarters.

Now, through our history lessons we know medicine in the Elizabethan era was, how shall I put it? Rudimentary? The monks, whilst putting their faith in the Almighty, found God to be working in all that surrounded them. Their use of herbal and plant-based medicine was very similar to the homeopathic tinctures which are so popular amongst those who choose to tread a different path to modern conventional medicine. The combined power of nature with its creator is, indeed, a potent healer.

The first few days were precarious; Sir Walter clung on to life. On more than one occasion the monks who were tasked with treating him and watching over him, called for the Abbot as they truly believed he had entered his final moments. But they were mistaken and glad to be so. The tenacity, resilience (such a popular word and much desired attribute craved by many today) and, dare I venture, his bloody-mindedness, saw Sir Walter gradually, day-by-day and week-by-week, regain his strength. Of course, when I say he regained his strength, what I really mean is that he turned away from death's door and retraced some of his steps. He was in a better condition than when providence stepped in and allowed the monks to find and rescue him.

That much was abundantly clear. However, he was by no means the same physical specimen who had set out, we believe, for the Himalayas. Oh no, his body had suffered tremendously; his face had aged and could most accurately be described as wizened. His powerful, muscular physique had wasted away and, whilst he retained an erect posture, he appeared, well, frail. His flesh may have weakened, but the same couldn't be said of his spirit. If anything, his harrowing and tortuous experience had left him with greater zeal and a reinvigorated faith in his God. This, more than their efforts and his physical rebirth, filled the monks' hearts with joy. God had given them their purpose and they had willingly accepted the challenge, allowing their Lord to work his wonders through their industry.

Almost three months to the day after he was carried over the threshold of their remote dwelling, Sir Walter was able to rise from his bed, unaided, and take his first, ponderous steps on the journey to a complete recovery. Every day he tested himself that little bit more; pushing himself harder, often against the words of his healers. On occasions, he pushed too hard and set himself back a few days. But he learned, accepting that time was not the severe and demanding mistress it had been to him in his days of adventure. Nor, indeed, was it the voice which had rebuked and ridiculed him as he passed his days in pension at the Elizabethan court. A minor setback was something from which to learn and realise his own limitations.

He would spend hours in the chapel, praising and thanking God. He worked in the kitchens, happy to serve all those around him. He learned to bake good bread and brew strong, sweet mead. Also, he mastered a darker ale whose burnt hop taste lingered mischievously upon the tongue and whose strength stealthily and seductively stole the power of speech and controlled movement much to the astonishment of the bewildered drinker. He laboured in the washhouse, insisting on doing the greater part of the laundry of the monastic order.

He was afforded regular periods of reflection and contemplation with the Abbot. The head of the order was an elderly, gentle figure who held a natural air of calm and reassurance. Sir Walter found it easy to talk with him and always left this company feeling comforted and strengthened in his belief in the higher, benevolent power that had sought to save him. It was, however, during one of these such counsels that their talk turned to what road lay ahead for Sir Walter.

The Abbott never pushed him; he was a very good listener whose very presence encouraged whomsoever was speaking to him to unburden their trouble or confusion. And his skill was in allowing them to reach a conclusion which felt like they had found it themself.

"If God has saved me, he must have a purpose in mind," Sir Walter reasoned. "And it must, surely, be to help spread his word and his glory, mustn't it?" Whilst the question had been shaped and delivered to his friend and confidant, it became rhetorical as the Abbot merely smiled and his eyes encouraged Sir Walter to continue.

"And to do so, I must leave," he concluded, his head dropping in sorrow. Nonetheless, he knew he had voiced what he needed to do and, whilst the Abbot himself inwardly would confess to feeling a great sadness at Sir Walter leaving their homestead, his countenance did not betray such thoughts. Both men knew that Sir Walter's destiny lay away from the sanctuary in which they shared their communion. With a heavy heart, Sir Walter looked up and, thanking the Abbot graciously, requested his permission to leave and return to England.

The Abbot agreed; he knew this was the inevitable outcome. He had known all along, once Sir Walter had been saved. But he also knew that Sir Walter had to make this decision himself.

"Sir Walter," he said, in a warm and gentle voice, "You have been a most welcome and inspiring visitor. We have been graced by your presence and it has allowed us to see the miracles that our Lord may perform. You have determined that it is now your duty to give this knowledge and strength to others. I believe you are right and, whilst we will all be very sad to see you leave our company, you do so with our blessing and fervent prayer for success in your ministry to others." The Abbot then added a personal request. "But before you go, I would ask of you one thing."

Sir Walter eagerly accepted whatever the Abbot asked of him, such was his joy, respect and gratitude.

"I would ask that you remain until the end of the month, nine days' time, at which we have our annual feast when we celebrate the life our Lord has given us and give him thanks for the bounties we have received."

Sir Walter began to babble, "B-b-b but I can't accept any more of your hospitality. Surely I can do something which will help you all for the months ahead?" his tone almost beseeching.

"Trust me," countered the Abbot, "your presence as a Guest of Honour at our feast will bring happiness and joy to all our community. Please say you will stay."

Overcome by the Abbot's humility, Sir Walter's voice broke with emotion as he readily accepted the offer. And thereafter, they continued their conversation, but this time it focused upon how Sir Walter would look to do God's work in the wider world. They talked for a long time and when Sir Walter was returning to his small cell after he had departed, he reflected on how much he would miss his conversations with the Abbot and how much he would miss life within the monastic walls.

As is so often the case, once a day for leaving is set, those days that remain pass swiftly. The precious mornings when he would help prepare breakfast; the hard gardening in the very large market garden, with its own distinct area for the growing and cultivation of herbs from which so many tinctures were made by Michael and Stephen; the oh-so-destructive and seductive aroma of the hops in the brewery…. He held tightly to them, wanting to hold them to him forever but, like sand, they just as readily slipped though his clenched fingers.

All too soon it was the day of the feast and he was banished from the kitchen areas as the Guest of Honour was not to know what delights were to be served that very evening.

Sir Walter took one last, long walk in the grounds which surrounded the monastery. As he always did, he found peace in the nature which surrounded him. Its calm restored him and told him that, whilst his sadness was to be expected, he was doing the right thing. He had work which lay ahead of him. Smiling, and nodding gently to himself, he resolved to return to his cell, offer early evening prayers and then get himself ready for the feast. In truth, the latter would not take long at all. He dressed in a plain habit as did every other fellow at the monastery, including the Abbot.

And so it was that he found himself seated next to the Abbot on the top table which, seemingly, was the only indicator of any form of hierarchy within the whole of the cloistered buildings and the behaviour of the monks. The Abbot was offered a natural respect, but it would also be true to say that this was how the brothers treated each other every day. The feast itself was a true banquet with each course complementing its predecessor. The diner was left with a feeling of complete enchantment having tasted exquisite dishes. The diner was satisfied, not wishing for a morsel more, but not feeling in any way replete. The wines and ale which accompanied the meal were also judged to perfection. Each goblet seemed to slip down more easily, leaving a velvet sensation within the throat which gradually turned to soothing warmth. All those present were intoxicated, but this was as much to do with the occasion and the culinary creations as it was the alcohol.

As they enjoyed the finest of their homemade cheeses accompanied by figs and apples from the orchard, the conversation flowed as easily as the very dark, heavy but enticingly sweet port. Then there came a loud rapping noise from the far end of the central trestle table, itself flanked by one to its right and its left. Sir Walter broke away from the conversation; indeed, all talk stopped as the figure of brother Ralph, whom Sir Walter knew well from his work within the bakery, slowly got to his feet. All eyes were upon him; he waited, seemingly milking the very moment, before speaking loudly and clearly so his voice could be heard by everyone within that great hall.

"Twenty six!" he declared, and promptly sat down. There followed a very clear and distinct ripple of laughter which flowed through the assembly. Louder in some areas, perhaps on account of the drink which some had consumed. Sir Walter turned a quizzical look towards the Abbot who returned his bewildered complexion with a polite, yet knowing, smile.

The monks fell back to their conversation and Sir Walter, not wanting to appear rude, chose to say no more. And yet, in little over 15 minutes there came another loud rap. Its volume was, perhaps, in part due to the fact that Brother Giles was seated not far from the top table, only three seats down on the table to the right of Sir Walter. He rose and with splendid timing as befits a positive orator, he declared, "Eight!"

The laughter, on this occasion, was louder and lasted longer. As an incredulous Sir Walter turned to his generous host he was, this time, met by a face still trying to overcome his mirth. The Abbot was unable to speak for all of half a minute and just as he appeared to be in a position to explain what was occurring, another rap rent the air and all turned their eyes to whence it came. Brother Simon was already on his feet, clearly unable to control his excitement. He strove hard to overcome the fit of giggling which was holding dominion over him, before blustering an audible "Fifty three!"

Brother Simon's mirth was matched by all. All, that is, apart from Sir Walter who joined in the laughter but was at a total loss as to what was happening all around him.

The Abbot took pity on him and, having first composed himself, spoke, a little haltingly to Sir Walter.

"My dear friend. Please let me explain. You see Brother Mycroft over there," at which point he gesticulated in the direction of the rather rotund and clearly proud, Brother Mycroft. Sir Walter knew him well, having learned the art of brewing sweet mead under his tutelage. "Well, about three years ago, Brother Mycroft had a wonderful idea. Aside from your good self, we have precious few visitors. Little from the outside gets to us. We are a close and friendly community, as you have found out. When it came to jokes we had plenty, but it did not take long for every single one of us to know all the jokes in circulation. People would begin, but would lose the attention of the listeners, who are naturally so polite, as they were all aware of their punchlines. So dear Brother Mycroft took it upon himself to write down every single joke and afford each its own number. His precious manuscript was copied and each copy was read and learned by all of our brothers. When it comes to our great feasts, what better way to conclude the evening than by telling jokes? A brother will announce his intention to offer his own favourite and then call out its number. The laughter which ensues reflects it current standing in the community."

"Amazing!" replied Sir Walter. "What a stroke of genius." He marvelled at the thought for a full minute as his genial host smiled at him.

Sir Walter then looked at the Abbot with a slightly mischievous look in his eye.

"Do you think as Guest of Honour, I could announce a joke? Would that be acceptable?"

The Abbot beamed at him. "But of course you may."

At this response, Sir Walter raised his tankard and swiftly consumed the ale which still lay within it, before grasping its handle firmly and rapping it upon the table in front of him. Silence quickly descended as everyone's eyes fell upon him. Sir Walter rose, surveyed his expectant audience before declaring with an emphatic cry, "Sixty seven!"

The quiet continued, was then slowly broken by laughter which began to rise and rise and rise. And then there was bedlam. The monks seemed to lose all sense of decorum, glasses of wine and port were spilt, tankards of ale were toppled, plates were knocked from the table. The sound of clattering cutlery would have been heard were it not for the howls of laughter which filled the hall. This went on for minutes. Sir Walter, feeling a growing pride, turned to the Abbot. But he was no longer seated next to him. A shuffling movement made Sir Walter look down to have his eyes met by the spectacle of the Abbot convulsed in merriment, almost unable to breathe, with his arms and legs flailing in the air. The actions of a dying ant came to Sir Walter's mind, but this ant was dying of laughter.

Sir Walter stood, turned and reached down to the Abbot, helping him to his feet and then ensuring he was seated safely. Still the Abbot and all around laughed heartily. He had turned puce and tears were streaming down his cheeks. Sir Walter hastily passed him some water and gently encouraged him to sip it.

Ever so slowly the Abbot's breathing returned to normal, but his sides were aching badly and his throat felt hoarse. Such had been the force of his laughter. Somewhat abashed, Sir Walter ventured, "I chose a good one there, didn't I?"

The Abbot became convulsed by giggles again, only just being able to splutter out "Oh yes, yes... we hadn't heard that one before!"

EPILOGUE

I had planned on writing the 'Perfect 10'. Let's face it, there is only so much wincing and shaking of the head that anyone can endure or, indeed, that you should inflict upon anyone. However, whilst compiling these tales, I saw a very short joke on one of the social media groups to which I belong. It did, indeed, make me wince and wear a very wry smile. But it also cried out for the 'pain' to be worthy of a longer introduction. This all occurred around the time of Liverpool FC being about to be crowned English Champions with all the preceding furore focusing upon what would happen should the remaining matches not be able to be played. A lot of 'past history' was played on many different channels and platforms. Watching one of these led me to consider developing this joke. As it does relate to past glories and TV commercials, it will sit better with readers of a certain age. However, the essence (scents?) of the tale remains accessible to all as does, perhaps unfortunately, its punchline.

So it's not been tried on any poor, unsuspecting classes of students. Only my son, Oliver, who, at 23 and sharing my passion and commitment for Preston North End, already knows more than enough about the pain and disappointment in football. Suffice to say his withering look and accompanying comment (which common decency prevents me from relaying to you) might just go to prove that this tale is worthy of its place in this collection?

THE SWEET SMELL OF SUCCESS

And so it transpires that Liverpool FC finally reclaims ownership of the title 'best team in England' by winning the Premiership in the somewhat strange season of 2019/2020. The history books tell me that it is the club's 48th major trophy and the same books tell me that this sustained success really had its beginnings in the 1960s, before growing at an alarming rate in the 1970s.

For those many people who are not football fans, this may mean very little. But the growing sense of expectation and constant exposure to the story in, seemingly, every form of the media did make it nigh on impossible to avoid in the year 2020.

Even prior to this, Liverpool FC players had graced the TV

screens in a series of adverts for the Nivea range of male skin products. And, perhaps, it's here where the secret of their success lies (taking nothing away from the work undertaken by a certain Mr Klopp).

The use of sports stars for endorsing cosmetics is not a new phenomenon. Let me take you back in time to an era when men's fragrance formed a very short list headed by Brut, Old Spice and Blue Stratos. Yes, the modern day male may purchase such with a sense (scents) of retro; their place in the market not quite keeping the same league as the fashion houses of Chanel, Yves St Laurent and Calvin Klein amongst many, many more.

But in the 70s, Brut was king. And sports stars pushed it to the consumer. British Heavyweight Champion, Henry Cooper, would 'splash it all over' (can't quite see the same strapline for the fine fragrances and at more than £50 a bottle for many, that's just as well). Barry Sheene, motorcycling hero, joined Henry. Indeed a few years later, Liverpool FC great Kevin Keegan shared the camera's eye with the boxing icon. In 1990, the darling of England's 'so near and yet so far' World Cup campaign, Paul Gascoigne, lent his image to help sell the famous green bottle.

But sporting stars selling Brut was not confined to the British Isles. 'Hollywood Joe' Namath - the famous quarter back of the New York Jets who masterminded the shock Superbowl triumph in 1971 - was another who was seen to wear, and suggest every man wears, Brut. And, finally, Mohammed Ali, world icon, could be seen to be an active promoter pulling no punches in his support of the product.

But in all this TV nostalgia, there is a lost story. And whilst one of their favourite sons, Kevin Keegan lauded Brut, it could, nay should, have been so, so different. For from 1973, the year the club won the old First Division and the UEFA cup, its marketing team had been working on an idea. To say that they were in the vanguard of thinking as to how a club could be run and actively use its assets would be a huge understatement but, somewhat tragically, they were just too far ahead of their time. You see, they too, were working on the idea of a fragrance... from Liverpool FC. Yes, there were hurdles as football, being so partisan, meant that a significant slice of the market would never, ever purchase such a product. That said, male fragrances were pretty much in their infancy and if they were clever in their marketing they could, they believed, capture a sizeable slice of that market. And with European success just achieved, and the hope for more, the market was a whole lot wider than just the UK. And, to add greater pathos to the tale, they were so right, with Liverpool beginning their domination of the European Cup in 1977. Had this marketing campaign worked and the product been launched.... How would things have turned out? That Liverpool FC was tremendously successful is a fact, but would they have been bigger still? Would the European market have opened up more readily? Could the money and exposure that would, undoubtedly, have come their way made a difference in their spending power? Would the leaner years of the nineties have been avoided?

Perhaps. Who can tell? But it didn't happen. The campaign fell at the final hurdle; all had seemed so very close to it becoming a reality. But why was this? What happened to prevent the launch of the *apres rasage* from Anfield? Well, it goes something like this.

The year is 1973. Bill Shankly is about to have overseen the club's first top flight league title success in almost a decade. The team will go onto win the UEFA Cup, a competition valued far higher than today's Europa League equivalent. Barry, John and Clare - to all intents and purposes, the marketing arm of Liverpool FC - were presenting their final ideas to the Board. I say final as the chairman and his close associates had been aware of the notion for some time and had been kept in the loop every step of the way.

The name of the fragrance had been tricky. Nothing too close to Liverpool as this would alienate a great many, but something which would be associated with the Liverpool brand. When Clare delivered their final suggestion, the boardroom fell silent.

The name 'Sharp Shooter' seemed to hang in the air, much like the big man up front, John Toshack. Now, by today's standards the name 'Sharp Shooter' would not really set pulses beating any faster. But please remember we are in the early 70s and marketing and advertising such commodities is in its infancy.

The room was suddenly alive with chatter. They liked it. Enthusiasm was clear on their excited faces. Clare, who had built up to her announcement very cleverly, and delivered the name in a most dramatic manner, heaved an internal sigh of relief and sat down. 'Job done' she thought. With one exception.

They had the product; they had the name; they had the brand; they had the backing. What they didn't have was the 'star' to be the face of the advertising campaign.

Bill Shankly, who was present at the meeting, was quick to decry the use of any of his players in the campaign.

"None of yer fancy dan feelings are getting into their heads!" he said, in a forceful manner. "This is Liverpool FC not some stage and screen school," his thick Scottish brogue adding emphasis to his claim.

"Absolutely Mr Shankly. Wouldn't have dreamt of it. And, also, they are too Liverpool. Just like the name can't be a direct attachment to the club, neither can the advertising show such a direct link. We need a strong male figure, but we need one which reaches beyond our shores," John explained.

Barry continued. "We're going to break into Europe. We want a name and a face which is recognisable everywhere and is that sharp shooter. Someone who embodies our brand; quick of thought and deed, powerful, reliable, stands apart from the rest...." His voice tailed off as he suddenly knew the answer.

"Yul Brynner," he muttered. Then he leapt to his feet and cried out "Yul Brynner!"

Once again it was Bill Shankly who spoke first.

"What in God's name can the guy from 'The King and I' bring to the product? Great musical, but not us."

"Er, Bill, 'The King and I' was 1954. This is 1973. He has been in films since then."

But Bill was already on his feet, demonstrably upset. "He may stand apart but that's because he was a King. There's singing: we don't sing. He spent all the film being chased by that woman: that doesn't suggest focus." Bill continued to reel off reasons why Yul Brynner was not the man, his arms folded across his chest and all Clare would hear were the words 'etc, etc' coming from their manager's mouth. She was in her early 30s but she had seen the film and, despite the rather heated atmosphere, she had to supress the beginning of a smile which twitched at the edges of her lips. Mr Bill Shankly was, unconsciously, doing a passable impression of Brynner's King Of Siam, albeit in a gravelly Scots accent which would have totally bemused Deborah Kerr's governess.

The chairman stood up, raised his hand and said, "Bill, Bill, calm down, man. It's not 'The King and I', it's 'The Magnificent Seven' isn't it? He was a sharp shooter in that. What a man, what an image. This could be our guy." The Chairman was often a man of few words, but when he did speak everyone listened. He liked the idea of Yul Brynner and his enthusiasm and confidence seemed to spread.

Bill Shankly had unfolded his arms and was beginning to nod. "Aye, I hadn't thought about that one. You have a point." He wasn't known for backing down; this was a pivotal moment and it was now that Barry played his ace.

"All true and a really good point, Mr Chairman. And I had considered that, but we can build on his latest film."

Blank faces turned towards him.

"On my recent trip to New York and San Francisco, gaining insight into campaigns and how after shave, or should I say *apres rasage*, is sold, I saw his latest film. I can't see how I didn't think of it before.

"Westworld!" he exclaimed. "It's a futuristic theme park and Yul Brynner plays a robot gunslinger who goes rogue. He's deadly. A true 'Sharp Shooter.' He is our man. A tough, non-nonsense, get it done and take no prisoners kind of man." Barry's eyes gleamed. Clare and John seated either side of him, grabbed his hands, tears pricking their eyes. They'd nailed it.

The board room was alive. Everyone was a gun slinger as they raced each other to draw their imaginary Colt 45 from their equally fictitious holster before offering their varied opinions of how the gun would sound when it was fired. Laughter rocked the room.

Now. All that was needed was the cooperation and involvement of Mr Brynner. Which actually meant the cooperation, involvement and payment of his agent.

The marketing trio was tasked with securing the Hollywood star's signature. An extraordinary Board meeting would be held in exactly one week's time.

"Surely it could only boost the film's appeal on these shores, too?" mused Clare. "It's too good to be true," she continued, before wishing she hadn't thought that.

Johan Graf was a surprisingly affable chap. It came as a bit of a surprise to John, who was the person deemed best to shape negotiations, that Yul Brynner's agent was Austrian. It mattered not, of course. And Johan was also excited. He had read what he had been sent all about the product and how it would be advertised. He could see his client as the face. He could also see a whole lot of money.

"John. Leave to me. Mr Brynner like this. I'm sure." He spoke in a clipped, broken English. John found himself thinking that he understood this better than when the great Bill Shankly got excited. Grinning to himself at this thought, he bade farewell to Johan, agreeing to talk again, whenever was good for Johan, before the Board meeting. Three such phone calls occurred, each one delivering more positive news. Johan knew that Yul Brynner not only knew something about 'soccer', but he was aware of the success of Liverpool FC. But he was still on location shooting his current project so couldn't speak to Johan.

"But, John, Yul will be very positive. He like England. He like football. He know Liverpool." All that was needed to cross the line was the signature.

It was a very unusual way to go about things, but with the Board members having very busy business lives, the meeting couldn't be bounced. They had been kept up-to-date with the communications and negotiations but on this Tuesday morning in early spring, they sat around the table as the line to Johan was dialled by John. There was so much expectation.

"Hi Johan, John here. With all the board. How are you? He enthused.

"Ah John. Good to hear you. But I am not happy. Neither you," Johan's tone, albeit naturally deadpan, allied to his few words did not make for a good feeling.

The others couldn't hear but could tell that things were not going to be as smooth as they had hoped.

"What's wrong?" cried John, a feeling of desperation running through him as he could sense a once-in-a-lifetime opportunity slip from his grasp.

"Ah John. It not easy. I was not knowing," came the defensive reply.

"Please tell me. What is it? What's wrong?" he couldn't hide his disappointment and desperation. Johan's brief words filled his ears and he simply closed his eyes and lowered his head. Without realising it, he had handed the receiver to Clare who stared at him, dumbfounded.

"What's wrong man?!" exclaimed Bill Shankly. "Tell us!" he demanded.

"The Chairman leant towards him, nodding. "We've got to know, lad. What's happened?"

John raised his head, his face a picture of misery as he repeated Johan's explanation to the room.

"Yul never wear cologne."

Printed in Great Britain
by Amazon